VINDICTA

THE LIQUIDATOR WARS
BOOK 1

KINDRA SOWDER

&

P. MATTERN

ISBN: 978-1-947584-88-4

This edition published by Kindra Sowder Media and P. Mattern, in 2024, in the United States.

DEDICATED TO:

Our ever present readers and those who love the macabre, for without you there's just too much damn light.

–K & P

VINDICTA

The Liquidator Wars
Book 1

Kindra Sowder

P. Mattern

CHAPTER ONE:
OH, DEATH

Calyx couldn't believe how cold Brynn was already, her pale skin drenched in the blood and sweat from the fight that brought upon her untimely death. As Calyx knelt beside her, a tear welling up in just one bright green glowing eye, she felt the wind kick up dust and debris from within the dark and damp alleyway.

She had fought well. The three bodies on the ground in the passage around them were a testament to that, but one got the upper hand and shoved a dagger into the underside of her ribs attempting to reach her heart. Vampires didn't turn to ash as they did in the movies when they died. The only way to be certain she had indeed perished was to wait for her resurrection. Brynn always cherished the safety of others more than her own, even if it meant an agonizing death.

She hadn't even taken a moment to

think about her safety as she fought valiantly against the enemy, exchanging blow for blow with speed and deadly accuracy.

The Liquidators were all that stood between them and absolute freedom from war, doing all they could to prevent them from attaining their ultimate goal. To rid the world of their kind and live in peace so the vampire race could flourish once more instead of being this sniveling and terrified race they are now. To coexist amongst the humans once again.

After what felt like an eternity, Brynn's body gasped, shocking Calyx. She stumbled back as she crouched next to her.

With one labored, gasping breath, she rose to a sitting position. Calyx nearly fell ass-first onto the ground from her crouched position. Brynn placed her hand over her heart. It hammered within her ribcage as she turned to her companion, red eyes ablaze with life and flashing a sapphire blue.

"Damn, that was close," Brynn said, still stunned as the gaping wound in the center of her belly right below her lowest rib began to close.

The Liquidator she slayed first fell to the ground with what the others perceived as Brynn's final death. The pain was excruciating, but she had suffered more at the hands of the Liquidators before so this wound was nothing compared. That was a much closer step to death than any other attempt had been.

"You don't say," Calyx snapped as she

2

stared at her, eyes narrowing with disapproval. "Don't do that shit ever again. You hear me, Daughter of Electi? I know you can take on two of them with no problem. The third one got his licks in coming from behind and managed to get past your awareness and defenses."

Brynn chuckled and took a deep, relaxing breath to slow her heartbeat as she dismissed Calyx with a wave of her hand.

"Yeah, yeah. Whatever you say."

She rose to her feet, brushing the crumbled bits of dried leaves off her leather slacks and sighed with relief. As she straightened, she saw the twins, Tarren and Bayn, striding toward her and Calyx. Neither of them looked pleased. Bayn frowned, and Tarren was positively scowling as he wiped black sticky Liquidator blood from his dagger, slinging it to the ground. They stalked toward them with animal ferocity, their distinct male scent wafting in the air toward them from down the alley. When they finally stood before the women, Tarren looked Brynn in the eye.

"Brynn," he said, looking down at her from his full height of seven feet and struggling to keep his tone light as he chided her. "Remember, just before you decided to attack the horde of Liquidators someone shouted at you, *Wait*? Well, that was me. I know you heard me. I was trying to spare you a death. Why is it that you always think you know best? Anyone's timing can be off. That was unnecessary."

3

By the time he finished, he had dropped the nice guy act and came across as completely baffled and put out with her. She couldn't say she blamed him. In the massive city of Los Angeles, she understood exactly why he hated the fact that she ran off on her own so often. Fighting the Liquidators in the city was already tough enough, but was even harder when she didn't listen to her men. Which was a common occurrence. She could say she came by her stubbornness honestly. Her mother had been known for the same trait quite well throughout the community when she was alive.

"Sorry, not sorry," she said, looking up at him unblinking and wishing she were taller. "I appreciate your concern, but I couldn't let anything throw my rhythm off. How many times do I have to tell you that warfare is a dance? It has a rhythm, and every move must be deliberate and timed precisely. Those that dance well survive—"

"Those that let their rhythm become broken, invariably perish," Tarren finished, interrupting her completely with a sarcastic sneer on his face.

Tarren looked to his identical twin Bayn for help, begging with wide eyes while attempting to look as if he wasn't at all. When his brother barely blinked, his shoulders sagged, and he opened his mouth.

"She never listens to me. Can you try to talk some sense into her, brother?" he pleaded.

4

Bayn smirked, his eyebrows rising in amusement.

"Well, she is our Queen and Brigade Leader. I think she knows that you speak out of concern. She is tough, brother. There is no arguing with her when she managed to leave the bodies of three Liquidators on the ground, now is there?"

Tarren went quiet, brooding as Brynn gave an impromptu curtsey, trying to keep her laughter in check and the grin from her face. She adored the Craven Twins, and they were invaluable in battle — almost as much as Calyx was. They were smart, cunning, and fast, knowing their way around any weapon they put their hands on. Because all of them knew what they were doing, they made a formidable phalanx during battle along with others of her comrades-in-arms.

Tarren would always try to go all *big brother* on her. As annoyed as she was with his insistence to treat her like a younger sibling, she knew it was because he loved her. The twins and Calyx, along with her little sister Gwenyth, were the only real family she had ever known after the death of their parents. That left her to lead the House of Electi against the Liquidators. To protect them and ensure their race would survive.

Suddenly, Brynn whipped around, her long hair twirling in an arc through the smog-laden air. She knew she had forgotten something.

"Oh, shit," she said. "The Quaji. I need

5

to hurry. I can feel them slipping away."

Digging into the small suede bag on her waist, she pulled out a small glass vial with a cork stopper and ran to one of the fallen Liquidators. She knelt on the blood-soaked concrete at his side. Brushing her hair back from her ear, she leaned down and listened for his last breath. It was the only sign of the Quaji leaving their body besides the soft snap and emerging light.

She saw the soul spark as it ascended. She possessed what the Mages called the *Sapphire eye* which made it clear to her when the last spark of life left the body and began to ascend toward the Heavens. Quickly, she brushed her hand through the air guiding it into the vial. She had to be very careful never to touch it for fear of contaminating it with her blackness, but she had been doing this since childhood and was well practiced.

She went around to the other bodies, listening carefully as each one spoke to her in its deafeningly silent way. The second of the fallen must have died while she was still fighting for her life, but she did manage to retrieve the soul of the third without issue.

Still on one knee, she held her captured treasures within the three vials up to the waning darkness of night. Inside each, something that moved and sparkled with a prismatic luminescent glow. It was something eternal and could be easily reanimated — not by her, but by a Mage skilled in the highest of the magical arts.

A soul spark was the basic description of what she held in her hands, and it was the only hope they had of replenishing their ranks without turning humans. That was something they were attempting to avoid even though the humans largely outnumbered them. The war between vampires and Liquidators waging just under the surface of what the human beings were aware of had taken its toll on the vampire ranks. Brynn hoped it would not remain that way. As long as fertile females within their race could continue to breed, there would be no need to get the humans involved. So, the Quaji was precious, and she cradled it to her chest right above her heart.

She sensed a warm hand on her shoulder, and turned to see Calyx standing behind her while the twins hung back to allow them their moment of privacy and understanding. The sun peeked just over the horizon, throwing a beautiful mixture of pinks, oranges, and crimsons into the morning sky. She felt the familiar buzz within her bones that alerted them to the rising sun. It was a hum that moved through her and down into the ground beneath her knees. The others undoubtedly felt it too. The sight of it along the cityscape almost made her stop in awe.

So beautiful, yet so deadly to her and her kind.

"We've gotta go. The sun is rising," she whispered as she looked down at Brynn, her eyes studying her friend as Calyx's green eyes glowed with the power of the rising orb.

CHAPTER TWO:
HOUSE OF ELECTI

Even with the sun rising and the thrum of its power moving through her bones, Brynn moved through the School of the House of Electi with purpose. Her blonde hair was streaked with red, flowing behind her like a cape and reaching to her swiveling hips. The walls of the tunnel were cut out of jagged rock, the location being the abandoned nuclear escape tunnels in Los Angeles.

The humans said, according to the miracle of the internet, that they didn't lead anywhere. That wasn't true at all. Because of their close work with the Fae, the Fae had enchanted the school that the House of Electi built to shield it from the human eye. So, it didn't matter how many times they walked through the expanse of twists and turns. They would always find nothing and be led out back into the waking world, the school only being visible to those magically inclined.

9

The suede bag that held her small glass jars weighed heavily on her hip, the weight of what she truly carried inside nearly crippling seeing as she was charged with the Quaji because of her gift.

The light that led them through the tunnels was dim since vampires didn't need a lot of light to be able to see perfectly. Having the night vision of an African cat helped, but passing through it did cast strange shadows on the walls as if they were truly creatures of the evening that attempted to follow her into the school. The thought sent a chill up her spine.

She tugged at the lapels of her jacket, zipping it halfway up so no one could see she had nearly lost her life that night. As a daughter of Electi, she had been trained at this very school by the female they called Natalia. Her sister Gwenyth didn't partake in training because she did not want to be a warrior. Natalia used to fight alongside her parents all that time ago, but developed another rare gift among the vampire race, causing her to no longer be able to take her place in battle against the Liquidators.

Brynn came upon the large steel doors, the small metal column directly in the center of the giant tunnel blinking. A little red light showed that the door had not been activated since classes ended. Without a moment's hesitation, Brynn placed her fingertip on top of an empty hole directly below the flashing light on the top of the tall cylinder that rose to her belly button. There was a small metallic click and then a strong pinch in the pad of her fingertip, causing her to hiss and her fangs to elongate because of a quick, stinging pain. She removed her finger and let the mechanisms inside of the cylinder go to work, testing her blood against the database of all DNA signatures within the race. She placed her finger inside her mouth and licked the wound. Her saliva would begin the clotting process. As she licked a few more times, the coppery taste reminded her that she had not fed in over a month. She would need to soon if she had any hope of having the strength to continue to fight.

With an electric thrill, the light changed from a blinking red to a steady green. The doors clicked open so she could enter the school. Once she walked through the doors, they closed behind her. The walls of the long hallway were white, clean, and pristine — sterile even — as she made her way to the only room she would ever need in the entire school after leaving it. There was a particular storeroom for the Quaji, holding all possible security measures to ensure the they remained unharmed.

The door wasn't in the main hallway, though, seeing as they wanted it as safe as they could make it. So, it was housed in the school's very center with at least three different types of security mechanisms, including the same blood testing cylinder that was at the main entrances along with solid steel doors laced with massive locking bars and a retinal scanner. This was to ensure that not only was the person entering a vampire, but that they were allowed to be within the room in the first place.

Brynn's *Sapphire Eye* made hers the most unique, being the only vampire in the entire race with not only rods and cones, but also another part of the retina that looked like a starburst. This was what made it possible for her to see the soul spark.

She made it to the designated room in record time, keeping one hand on the strap of her suede pack just on the chance someone attempted to act brave and grab it. Even though the place was nearly empty because it was daylight, she was always extremely cautious. Some would even say overly cautious, but it was her philosophy never to risk the Quaji. That meant, if it hadn't been placed within the confines of the room, she would have her hands on it at all times.

She stood in front of the solid steel door and put her finger on the blood tester, feeling the same sting as before. The light turned green to release the retinal scanner from within the wall. A metal ring circled her head, a small laser ejecting from the arm that turned it as a red light shone into both of her eyes. It stung slightly, but that was only because she was weak and hadn't fed. Even a little bit of light was too strong for her delicate vision. After another moment, the laser turned green, and the bars began to slide out of their home within the door, the large mass of metal swinging open to allow her entry.

Her booted feet crossed the threshold, the chill in the air nearly palpable as she stepped inside. A shiver moved up her spine, but she suppressed it as best as she could. The room that stored the Quaji was rather large with shelves built into the stone walls instead of lining the floor to ensure the stability of the structure that held them. They could not risk the Quaji being smashed on the ground in the event of an earthquake.

She ran her fingers along the shelves in an attempt to find three empty spaces to place her newest conquests. Three Liquidator Quaji were her spoils of the fight in the alley, and because she nearly died, they had almost slipped away into the ether of the afterlife. Once resurrected, they would have no memory of their lives as Liquidators. They would only recall their new vampire flesh and their vampire blood, the craving hitting them as soon as they were corporeal, causing them to have to feed immediately.

Brynn finally came to an opening among the crowded shelves and began to dig inside her bag, feeling around for the slight warmth of the Quaji inside its glass prison. Her fingertips brushed the mild heat and she wrapped her hands around the three small, warm, and tingling jars. She placed them in the open space, lovingly stroking one of them with just her pointer finger.

"Hello, Brynn, Daughter of Electi," a soft

feminine voice came from the doorway, causing Brynn to turn her head to see her company.

Natalia floated into the room and toward her, her long, silken blue nightgown brushing the ground as she moved. She stopped in front of Brynn, her head tilting to the side as if she sensed something, her graying eyes no longer able to visualize after becoming an Oracle. Only her mind's eye was open now, and it knew all.

"You could have taken the Quaji home with you and waited until the sunset, my dear."

"I know, Natalia, but..."

"You were fighting again," she gasped and gripped Brynn's arm, squeezing hard. "You nearly suffered the final death tonight, warrior. You know we cannot risk losing you to the Liquidators. You are far too precious."

Brynn didn't move, only froze as she stared at the older woman. She was over five hundred years old and still looked no older than fifty, but you could see that her gift was taking its toll on her body as crow's feet appeared at the corners of her eyes.

Brynn nodded. "I know, I know. We cannot collect the Quaji to replenish our ranks without the *Sapphire Eye*. I try to be care—"

"That does not matter. It is not only the *Sapphire Eye* we must protect. We must ensure your survival as well, as a Daughter of Electi. We cannot lose any more of our people."

Brynn placed her free hand on Natalia's shoulder, letting the warmth of what she had just been holding in her hand move through the woman's thin flesh to reassure her.

"I am sorry, Natalia. I know we must protect our ranks, but I can't just sit back and watch us fall to the Liquidators. I am avenging those who have fallen to their will, and I will not stop until every slayer is dead."

Her other hand rose to cup Brynn's cheek, shaking as her eyes squeezed shut like she was attempting to close herself off to something. A vision maybe, but Brynn could feel the thrumming of the sun's power becoming stronger the longer she stood there with the female. When she opened them again, her irises were completely white. Brynn's image reflected in them, Natalia's eyes wide with anxiety and exhaustion.

"Your thirst for vengeance will one day be your undoing, Brynn. I hope your soldiers won't be too late."

"You don't have to worry," she reassured Natalia in a soft tone. "I want to see it. That is if you don't mind."

Natalia smiled at Brynn and glided across the room on nimble feet, moving to the far wall. She brushed her hand over its smooth white expanse with love and pride. The wall moved slightly and then began to slide into the stone surrounding them, exposing the

15

experiment she and Brynn had been working on for months. Something Brynn told her soldiers would give them a significant advantage in the war against the Liquidators.

This operation had started as an idea, not anything concrete despite the fact that the Electi possessed some of the most advanced technologies known to the magical world. And this was indeed magic, the fusing of the supernatural and scientific.

It was something Natalia was insanely proud of as was the eldest Daughter of Electi. She felt the young vampire's excitement flutter inside her chest as the wall opened up to allow them entrance into the lab.

Brynn walked into the room, taking in the familiar sight of large glass tubes filled with synthetic amniotic fluid to ensure the survival of the embryos. The two women had worked tirelessly to create the creatures that grew within the glass and metal homes. Both women moved to stand in front of the one they were most satisfied with. Even though Natalia couldn't see in the literal sense, her mind's eye had proven to be quite useful in managing the world around her.

A bird-like face framed large, closed eyes as a long beak protruded from its center. Massive wings folded against its enormous body, covered in paper-thin leathery wings. They were so much like the creatures that roamed the Earth eons ago, but different in one way in particular.

Vampire blood had been infused into

them along with the magic of the Fae, making them a formidable weapon. The Zoo, as they had come to call it, was powerful and beautiful.

"She's almost ready," Brynn stated in a breathy voice filled to the brim with excitement.

"Oh, yes. Nearly there. I would say she will be ready to take flight in the next twenty-four hours. As well as five others. Your army is almost ready, and we are clear to implant another ten within seventy-two hours."

"Fantastic."

Natalia watched Brynn with her mind's eye, taking in her wide eyes and small knowing smile.

"Keep up the good work, Oracle. You are the true genius of the Electi."

CHAPTER THREE:
MADNESS RISING

Brynn stirred gently underneath twisted sheets in the darkened room, the substantial thickness of the blackout curtains, gray velvet lined with a triple layer of dark flannel shut out all the offending sunlight that caused her pale flesh to burn and smolder within seconds of exposure.

Across the expanse of the room, underneath a heavily silk-laden headboard on the opposite side, slept Brynn's sister Gwenyth. She was only a few years younger than Brynn, but held an aristocratic air making her seem much older. Gwenyth had her own well-appointed room in the mansion they were staying in built long ago by another family of their race. The home had been left to rot, but Brynn instantly fell in love with it the first moment she set eyes on the once majestic structure. She found that she couldn't let it go to waste. She snatched it from the real estate market quickly and remodeled and refurbished it to have the best that life in the modern world could offer.

Brynn couldn't sleep without being in proximity to her younger sister even though they both had their own bed chambers. She had always been Gwenyth's surrogate mother, nurse, confidant, and teacher. Gwenyth was growing into a striking beauty, but she had been marked with a disability that caused most entities that met her to avert their eyes, cluck their tongues sympathetically, or turn away in aversion once they noticed it. In particular, those of the aristocracy, which they were a part of not just because of Brynn's station, but also because of their family lineage.

Gwenyth had a withered arm, a very rare defect within the vampire ranks, but an anomaly, nonetheless. A clumsy delivery at birth had caused her left forearm and hand to become shrunken and wasted, very much in contrast to her smooth, creamy complexion and flawless figure. The rest of her was perfect, and Brynn felt sorry for her sister. She was worried she wouldn't be able to find someone worthy of her. There didn't seem to be a single man who looked her way because of the affliction that was in no way her fault, just something she has. Gwenyth acted as if it didn't bother her, but Brynn knew the harsh truth.

Brynn had long shielded her sister from speculative glances as best she could, but there was only so much one could do short of locking her away in their home. She'd been seven years old when Gwenyth was born and remembered the joy, bustle, and anticipation of the birth of her wealthy parent's second child. She had even been excited about the new arrival.

Then there was the sad hush that followed, followed by the unveiling of the hideous appearance of the newborn's arm sucking the air out of the chamber like a vacuum. It was something Brynn had never seen no matter how others spoke of it. When she was a child, she felt as if it made her sister special and never recognized the handicap as such. That didn't stop the whispers of others who quickly dismissed her as soon as she walked into a room. Even with Brynn at her side, she was always treated as an outcast. That certainly didn't change with their parents death. If anything, it worsened.

It was then that they both became the wards of her Uncle Vincent who insisted Gwenyth wear a thick glove over her withered arm at all times. Though the glove was nicely made and bejeweled, it only served to stigmatize Gwenyth even more.

When Brynn confronted her uncle, demanding that Gwenyth be allowed to dispense with the glove, he became irate.

"This is my house," he told her as she stood before him, her cheeks flushed with indignation on her little sister's behalf. "I cannot and will not tolerate the display of anything that speaks of weakness or imperfection. Your sister has a lovely face and form, but they are all eclipsed by her withered appendage. Do you realize what a huge dowry I will have to offer to make certain she marries well?"

Brynn had bristled for Gwenyth's sake at her uncle's harsh diatribe.

"We are nonetheless true Daughters of the Electi. The Chosen Ones. How dare you insinuate that my sister is something less?"

She couldn't stop the words as they rushed from her lips, containing the harsh tones of disdain that she barely attempted to hide.

The blow came suddenly, splitting her bottom lip and causing blood droplets to fly into the air between them. The taste of iron hit her tongue and flooded her mouth.

It was the first time living as his ward her Uncle had ever struck her, and the last.

"Go girl!" he had thundered, towering over her. "I see you have inherited your mother's sharp tongue. That is unfortunate. Remove yourself from my sight and never question me again. Gwenyth will wear the glove, even on her wedding night. No male entity wants imperfection in his bride. She will wear it, or I will lock her away."

Brynn turned onto her side as she pushed the thoughts away, looking toward the darkened window to her right and sighing with irritation. The ghosts of the past always visited her when she was supposed to be resting. Sleep was always an issue, her thoughts always running rampant with what her life was then and what it had become.

When she was born, they realized she had a gift that was even rarer than any physical defect within their race. The gift allowed her to see the Quaji of those close to or at death's door. The *Sapphire Eye* was something that had been coveted by many for centuries, but only surfaced in a rare few, including her. Sometimes she even wondered if it was truly a curse wrapped in the guise of an extremely deceptive gift. She had been told multiple times that she should feel grateful a higher power saw fit to place this gift upon her shoulders, but she always felt weighed down by it. She only truly appreciated it once since she realized its purpose. That didn't keep her from realizing the preciousness of the Quaji, though, knowing it could replenish their population if only she could locate the Mage that could replenish them. Only he could convert them into the forms they desperately needed, and she had been searching the texts for years in an attempt to learn his location and identity, but failed in her attempts so far.

She rolled onto her back, moaning because the gentle hum within her bones marked the time at around noon. At this rate, she knew sleep would escape her as it had a tendency to do and she should at least do something useful with her crippling insomnia. Instead, she decided that she needed rest and closed her eyes with a reluctant sigh.

She finally drifted into a state that floated somewhere between full wakefulness and the sound restorative sleep that her war-torn body desperately craved when she heard a tapping on the door. As she turned toward the sound, Bayn burst in, breathing ragged with urgency in his wide eyes.

"Apologies, Daughter of the Electi," he said, a look of seriousness on his face. "There is a breach in the far Quadrant and four fatalities already. It is a small contingent of Rogues of some sort that we have never seen before, clad in black leather with hoods over their faces. They are fierce fighters."

Brynn immediately sat up and turned her back to Bayn. He averted his eyes as she shucked her sleeping gown down from her shoulders to her waist, donning first a leather vest and then a leather tunic over it. Kicking the gown away, she pulled up leather breeches and stout boots,

"How do you know they are Rogues?" she asked.

Bayn turned around again. His face reddened. He'd never understood Brynn's lack of modesty. He and Tarren had been infatuated with her from the time they first met. Not only because of her careless, wild beauty, but also for her courage. But, damn, didn't she know what the occasional glimpses of her half-naked body could do to a man?

24

"Wait," he said, daring to grab Brynn's arm as she walked past him. "You haven't had anything to drink, and you are still healing. As always, I am honored to be of service."

Brynn looked for a moment as though she'd like to refuse, but finally, her shoulders sagged in resignation.

"I know you're right, and Calyx would insist anyway. I do feel the Thirst and need the energy, but let's hurry."

Bayn kept his composure though the excitement he felt at the thought of Brynn feeding from him welled up from his inner core. He unbuttoned his shirt in the front so she could have access to his throat and well-muscled chest. She hesitated only a few seconds before pulling him closer and sinking her fangs into one of his well-defined pecs.

Bayn experienced a sort of euphoria as she fed, as well as many sexual stirrings. The thought of her perfect cupid bow mouth on his skin thrilled him.

He would gladly have let her drain him, but the feeding was over too soon. Brynn was all business as she wiped a blood droplet from the corner of her mouth and licked her finger.

"Thank you," she said brusquely. "Now, tell me what you know of these attackers."

"They displayed no Sigil," he told her. "No emblem of any house and no coat of arms or crest or flag of any territory or creed. Our troops are readying now, and we must hurry because they have set a fire at every point where our slain have fallen."

"Very well then," Brynn said, glad to be moving around. "But we know they are the enemy, because of the hour they have chosen to attack us. Most likely Liquidators that have decided to act on their own. Please have three of our Elite Guard stay behind to guard my sister."

"As you wish," Bayn affirmed as he turned and shouted to someone outside in the hall. "You two. Stay here with the sister."

"Yes, sir," two large males replied as they shifted into the room.

Gwenyth sleepily roused from sleep because of the racket and shouting.

Her eyes were wild with fright as she took in the two men that came to stand before her as she moved toward the threshold, her blonde hair matted to her sweaty forehead caused by the heat. Her blue eyes that reminded Brynn so much of her own shimmered in the darkness surrounding them, her fear palpable throughout the room as her mouth fell open in shock.

"Brynn? What's happening?" she asked as Brynn stood before her, placing her hand on her sister's to comfort and ease her.

Gwenyth pulled her nightgown closer to her chest in a display of aristocratic modesty. A real lady even in chaos.

Even though Brynn was fearful, she could not let her little sister see it. She was not the type to do so. She fought bravely, always showing a fierceness that frightened their enemies. Because she was a female, any enemy that met her was terrified of the long fangs and quick movements, always bowing down to her in the end. Especially those that belonged to the Liquidators' ranks.

"You will stay here with these men. You don't have to worry, sister." Brynn stood and turned to the men, pointing at Gwenyth as the next words left her lips. "She doesn't leave this room. Got it?"

"Yes, Daughter of Electi," both men whispered in response, lowering their heads briefly in fealty.

They knew that they must protect Brynn's younger sister from harm even if it meant their own deaths.

"You're not afraid, Brynn, but you should be," Calyx told her as they moved quickly through the hall and descended the twisting spiral steps from the upper rooms in tandem.

Their shadows moved along the clean white-blue with the dim light. Any more than this and it would hurt their eyes during the day.

"They have some sort of magic that summons flame, and they seem to be able to direct it. It is unnatural and dies after a short time, but can still inflict pain and damage. Plus, the sun is still out," Calyx continued.

"How the Hell do the Liquidators manage to get such things?" Brynn asked petulantly as they continued their way down, each step vibrating through her entire body just like the sun that hung high in the sky.

"I'm not sure, but as long as you can avoid dying again…"

Brynn turned to her friend, reaching to squeeze her hand. Calyx's glowing eyes were several shades deeper with concern.

"I promise not to die," Brynn told her. "You must promise me something in return."

They reached the massive oak door that opened to the outside. Tarren and Bayn were close behind them, but neither spoke a word. They waited to hear what Brynn would say to her lifelong friend.

"I know you are half Fae, but don't hover so much. Please? I can't concentrate on the fight if I sense you on my heels."

Calyx grinned and nodded.

"I know you are prepared, my Sister, my Sorror Bellator. Now that you have promised me, I know everything will be okay. You never break a promise."

Several of Brynn's Elite Guard fell in behind them. Brynn glanced behind her and nodded to several of them, including one of her newest recruits, Ryder Perkins.

He had shown up fighting on their side at a critical time during one of their skirmishes several months before. He was a vampire. Brynn could attest to that. He had the scent of all vampire males — a combination of seawater, stone, and musk. The scent that would fill your lungs as you stood on cliffs overlooking the ocean.

Tarren and Bayn had taken an instant dislike to Ryder and cautioned Brynn about trusting him, especially including him in the ranks of the Elite Guard. She passively dismissed their fears. He had fought long, hard, and successfully for their side ever since.

Still, she mused. Tarren and Bayn were right about one thing. Ryder was somewhat more than a vampire. When he'd told her his backstory she had sensed immediately that he was leaving something, or maybe several somethings, out.

The bottom line? She felt safer having him in their ranks rather than outside of them. If she spurned him, she reasoned that he would have to become a mercenary. She would rather have him fighting with them than against them.

Calyx agreed with her. Calyx had a pronounced sense of potential danger when it came to Brynn. She had assured Brynn that as far as Ryder was concerned, he would protect her loyally.

Still, the Twins never looked pleased to see him, merely nodding when they were in the same room, and making sure they gathered more tightly around Brynn and Gwenyth than usual as if they expected him to turn on her at any minute.

The heavy door flew open to unveil the commotion of dust, the flash of daggers and swords, and the coppery smell of blood. The sunlight filtered in, and they had not had a chance to prepare for the onslaught of rays. Their gear that had been enchanted by the Fae to help them go out in the sunlight in case of events like this still hung by the door. None of them had had a moment to slip the thin fabric over their exposed flesh before the doors opened and the assault began.

The Fae had always worked within proximity of the vampires because they shared one common enemy. The Liquidators were slayers, but they didn't focus on the evil of the world. They targeted everything supernatural in nature, even though they were cut from the same magical cloth. They were good once, their souls corrupted by evil. You could smell bitter and burned remnants of the souls that lingered within them.

Calyx was not affected by the sun because of her Fae blood, but Brynn felt the searing pain of it on her face and the side of her throat, causing her to cry out and flinch away from it as both Bayn and Terran ran for cover within the shadows. The remainder of her small troop, including Ryder, ducked away from it as quickly as they could.

Her hand rose to her face to shield it from further damage as she turned away and stumbled out of the foyer and into the living room to the left. Her energy zapped out of her from the injury and sudden contact with the sun's rays. Her knees nearly buckled, causing her to trip on the beautiful Oriental rug in the living room and fall to her knees beside the large glass and metal coffee table. She almost couldn't hear the steady thump of metal on wood as the weapons of their enemy penetrated their home, causing Brynn to think they definitely needed to see about modern security systems and weaponry. She had been trying to avoid them, but it looked as if they would have no choice, provided they survived this unwelcomed intrusion.

"Brynn," Calyx cried, kept at bay on the other side of the foyer by the mass of weapons barreling inside.

Brynn dropped her hand from her face despite the searing and debilitating pain, turning toward the voice of her friend and comrade. She couldn't make her out through the light, her eyes barely making the attempt to adjust to the brightness because of her injury. Once hit by the sun, even a minuscule amount, your body would turn all energies and blood supply to the area to speed healing, making it the most debilitating injury any vampire could sustain.

Brynn heard Calyx's voice over the harsh sounds of battle, as she raised one tiny fist above her head of curls and screamed, "Umbra!"

Immediately there was a hush as the sun temporarily dimmed, a shadow descending through the atmosphere and hovering like a pall over Brynn's part of Los

Angeles. It wasn't something that could be picked up on weather monitoring equipment, and only the Fae and angels and vampires would be able to see that the sudden dimming of sunlight was caused by a massive being of shadow, shaped roughly like a stingray.

Though Brynn's torture eased, she was immediately suffused with guilt. How many times had Calyx been forced to call upon such ancient magic on her behalf? There was a price attached to seeking their aid, and it was a price that Brynn never wanted Calyx to have to pay.

Freed from her torture by light, Brynn stood and stumbled into the fray.

CHAPTER FOUR:
BATTLE BORN

It was a blessing that few humans looked skyward anymore unless there was a bright light by night or a loud sound that alerted them to the presence of something sinister.

As the sun finally slid over the edge of the horizon, the Umbra that Calyx summoned to save Brynn from any more painful burns inflicted by the sun's glaring rays lifted. For those that had either the second or third sight, it floated away as if it had the subtle pectoral fins of a sea creature, graceful and silent. It blocked the emerging stars in vast areas of the night sky as it drifted away, turning the bright day into protective faux nightfall.

A battle cry rose from the Electi as the change transpired, making them feel joyous as the fight inside of them only grew and needed to be expelled through their shouts. This was the moment they had been waiting for. The moment when they could slay any Liquidator or traitorous fiend that entered their walls.

The enemy flew in from every direction, and occasionally a fireball arched through the air and hurtled toward them at blinding speed, crashing into the grounds, and lighting patches of grass aflame. Several of the Warriors were stationed near Brynn's home and armed with fire extinguishers, ready to put out any fires that ignited around the periphery of the mansion's extensive property. It had been an unusually dry season, spawning epic wildfires in the hills around Los Angeles, so the hedges and vegetation surrounding the old building caught fire instantly when the flames licked at them with greedy tongues. Startled cries floated into the empty sky, smoke and steam rising from it. It filled their lungs as they waged war against the enemy that had penetrated their walls. The mansion was surrounded by two large walls with entrance gates that required a code to get in, but somehow the Liquidators had managed to climb them or break the barriers completely to gain entry.

Calyx was instantly attacked by a youth wearing a black hood. A sheaf of blond hair hung over one eye, and the uncovered eye glowed phosphorescent green. She recognized the glowing orb instantly because she also possessed them within her skull.

"Turncoat," Calyx cried out, angrily believing that these traitors all needed to burn.

All but the most devious and reprobate

of the Fae Folk fought with the Electi, based on an ancient accord forged long ago when the Liquidators first emerged to slay an entire village. Calyx wondered momentarily why any creature with even a drop of Fae blood would fight on the side of the Liquidators seeing as they killed most other magical beings on sight even though they were also one themselves.

She soon had her answer. As the male entity raised his sword to deal her what was meant to be a death blow, she saw the permanent branding on the inside of his wrist. She immediately recognized the brand, which looked like a circle captured on the crest of a wave. It was meant to represent a bubble on the surface of the water. Unstable and unreliable.

Forsaken.

To have been branded this way meant the recipient had likely killed an innocent and was probably an escapee from an *Iron Slam* — a special prison for Fairies who had proven to be violent deviants. How any of the Fae captors there escaped was beyond Calyx, but she fought against him nonetheless, knowing she must kill him or die by his hand. She would not have the latter.

This recognition made Calyx even more determined that he would meet his death by her hand.

There was a loud clang as his sword hit her upraised blade. Before he could reverse his forward momentum to launch a second blow, she pushed the sharp edge of her sword across his face, ripping open the skin across the bridge of his nose and across his cheek to his ear. When he turned back to her after stumbling a few steps, his eyes were filled with rage, his mouth twisted into a growl as he gritted his teeth. Blood poured from the wound and Calyx smelled the foul and bitter evil within it in the air, causing nausea to roll in her gut.

"Focula," he swore in the Fae tongue, calling her a bitch.

Calyx then slid a jeweled dagger from a sheath along her waist. It was the silver one set with rubies and obsidian that Brynn had given her for her last birthday, and she adored it. Without a moment's hesitation, she drove it into his chest. She turned the blade up, letting him feel the agony of a blow that dealt the final death of an Electi and twisting it.

"Zbina et zbina daeca," she railed at him, watching with satisfaction as his blood ran in thick green streams, sparkling with the magic within it.

Her war cry was a common one and, roughly translated, meant, *Die, and die badly.* The youth slumped first to his knees, then fell to the ground face first as the blade slipped from the confines of his body. He was dead. She had felt her blade pierce his heart, stopping its incessant beating almost immediately.

Another clumsy attacker quickly occupied Calyx and was quite chaotic compared to the last one. She craned her neck through the dust to see Tarren shoving a sword directly down the throat of an enemy and then pulling it out in a gush of blood and entrails. The Twins' height advantage allowed them to develop their unique killing styles and every other individual within the Electi wanted so badly to learn, but never possessed the same gift of height. They were two of very, very few.

Near Tarren was Brynn, not allowing her height to detract in the least from her swordsmanship as she slashed and immolated any who came in proximity to her. She'd found that the fireballs being lobbed were magical in nature, and though they burned out, she had managed to snag a few as they flew above her head. She turned her sword into a flaming harbinger of death for a few valuable seconds before the flames subsided, slashing any Liquidator that dare approach her and leaving a slash of fire across their bellies as intestines spilled out of them and onto the beautiful lawn.

Brynn was determined to work her way to the imposing figure that stood not even twenty yards from her watching the fray. They were not only dressed head to toe in black, but also wore a black suede mask over their face. The mask had holes for eyes and metal cage work where their mouth should be. It glinted menacingly in the twilight of the magical shield of the night that Calyx had thrown over the city. They seemed to be protectively surrounded by a rotating circle of the fiercest warriors. With Bayn and Tarren at her side, she slowly advanced toward her ultimate target as the observer's eyes watched her. Studied her with incredulity and interest.

"Help me up," she demanded of Tarren as they came within a few yards.

Tarren grinned. He knew exactly what she meant. With one motion he swung her up on his shoulders where she stood with perfect balance, hair whipped by the wind, her eyes half closed against the gritty dust in the air but still able to make out her target perfectly through her lashes.

When the enemy ranks broke, and she had a clear shot at the menacing dark figure, she leaped, moving through the warm air with perfect grace.

The figure held a sword up and at an angle as they saw her catapulting toward them, but she surprised them by curling up into a ball in midair and coming in lower than anticipated. It was a beautiful, acrobatic move, and one of her favorites when she was faced with Liquidators, whose ranks often included giants of eight feet or more while few of the Electi's own ranks possessed this strength. Their men were large and built like warriors, but Tarren and Bayn were some of the tallest she had ever seen, towering over everyone.

On her way down, she sliced down her opponent's side, hoping to see bowels tumble out into the dust and grass. That part didn't go according to plan as her sword hit metal instead. The metal clang rang through her weapon, causing it to vibrate in her hands.

As a backup, she always had a dagger in easy access of her left hand. She quickly whipped it out and used it to plunge into their chest, causing blood to well up around it. She could tell at that moment it was a large man. He fell to the ground quickly. When she fell on top of him, she straddled his hips and continued to push down on the weapon, her fangs elongating with the joy of her kill. But he wasn't dead. She could sense it as his eyes stared up at hers.

Seeing him fall, his ranks broke and scattered in retreat, many of them picked off by the rest of her soldiers.

"Come on, Daughter of the Electi," Bayn said as he tried to lift her off the leader of the attack by gently pulling her up by her arm.

She grunted in frustration as Bayn then grabbed her around the waist to pull her back, but she wanted to know more about the man she had just attempted to slay.

"I'm fine, Bayn. Put me down."

He did as she requested, suddenly dropping her, and causing her to stumble. She recovered quickly and sauntered to the man's body on the ground. She removed her short dagger and stared at the wound she'd just inflicted, confused by what she saw once she did so. She kneeled beside the man and every instinct in her body told her to turn and run as far away from him as she could, but she resisted it. Her fangs began to throb because of the threat he presented.

She tried to figure out why the blood that seeped out of this creature was not the black blood of a Liquidator or the slightly green glittering substance from a Fae Turncoat, but the red blood of another phylum of being altogether.

"Wait," she said, holding up one small pale hand. "I want this enemy leader taken prisoner. Bind his wounds, but make sure he is chained. I will need to interrogate him as soon as I am able. I want to know who he is and where he came from."

Bayn squatted beside Brynn. He saw what she had been staring at for the first time, and he whistled, the sound low and haunting.

"Well, you nearly finished him off, Brynn," he said thoughtfully, staring at the motionless man. "I am not sure that he will survive this."

Tarren stopped next to his brother and mused, "Well, then. Maybe we should have a look under that mask, bother?"

Tarren bent down also and ripped off the marauder's mask. The head lifted and fell back on the ground, rolling to the side.

He was handsome. A sheen of sweat coated the beautiful planes of his face. He had full lips, a straight nose and black hair that splayed out against the dusty asphalt he lay on in the driveway.

"Have him taken into the basement,"

Brynn repeated, "If he dies from his wounds, it is no matter to me. He would have gladly cut me in two with his long sword. But have the surgeon tend to his injuries. If the Gods favor him, he will survive."

"As you wish, Daughter of the Electi," Tarren said, though Brynn could tell that his heart wasn't in it.

It was all right with Brynn that he kept his tongue.

She already got enough lectures from Calyx as it was.

With Calyx's help, and with all the Rogues that hadn't met Death on the battlefield retreating for all they were worth, Brynn set about capturing as many Quaji in her glass vials as she was able. It was quite a task, and there was no one else to do it. A contingent of her guard remained on duty, hovering over him as she moved past fallen body after body regretful of the waste of youth and energy.

"They will come back," she reminded herself, "to different lives and a different master because they will serve me."

It made her more determined than ever to find the Mage Resurrectionem, the only Mage in existence with the power of restoring the Quaji to living beings again.

Weary but finished at last, she wiped her hands on her blood-soaked shirt. She squared her shoulders and, after giving final instructions for the disposal of the corpses, she turned back toward her home. She was

looking forward to the victory feast, after
which Calyx, her voice high, true, and sweet
would play her Crwth and sing.

"Hurry," Bayn told Tarren after they had
showered and donned clean clothing. "She
won't want to be kept waiting, and I can smell
the food from here."

Tarren was completely nude, sprawled
sitting up at the headboard of his bed in the
quarters he shared with his twin, playing with
his iPhone. He had found a game on there he
loved to play, which baffled the other vampires
around him. They didn't take part in a lot of
the human games like he did, but this was
one of the few ways he was able to find relief
from stress.

"Relax," he told his brother. "Try to
develop some hobbies other than warfare, why
don't you? For instance, I find playing games
on my phone the perfect denouement to a
battle. I am addicted to playing *Vandal
Assassin*."

Bayn snorted in mock amusement and
began to dress, slipping on an elegant black
suit he only wore after a victorious battle.

"So, you relax and restore your war-torn
soul by playing make-believe war games?
Don't you think that's a tad ironic?"

"Not at all," Tarren said, still punching
buttons on the touch screen. "What else would
I be doing? Arranging flowers?"

"Well, not that, but maybe hooking up with someone? When was the last time you got laid, brother?"

Tarren smiled without looking at Bayn, still intent on killing imaginary vandals.

"Just a few days ago, as a matter of fact," he said smugly. "That new maid. The redheaded one. She started making my bed before she realized that I was still in it. She saw my magnificent rod having its morning stretch, and she climbed on. She didn't even ask my permission first. I was appalled, of course."

The fact that Bayn was about to lecture him wasn't lost on him.

"More like you drug her into your bed and convinced her to lie with you," Bayn joked. "You're making my point for me. You are too lazy to even meet someone outside of Brynn's house."

"You, my friend, are just jealous because you aren't getting the same caliber of maid service," Tarren shot back. "Let me turn it around and ask you when the last time you got laid. Hmmmmm? When was the last time you oiled your long sword? Hasn't it been a while? Shouldn't you be branching out? As far as I know, you haven't ever slept with anyone but fairies. Everyone knows they are not particular."

"I am saving myself, thanks," Bayn said testily. "For her. There is no one else for me, and you used to feel the same way, I recall. Are you out of the running now? If so, I am thrilled. I will marry her and pump her glorious belly full of my seed, and you will get to watch little mini me's running around with my face."

"Never," Tarren answered, taking a gamble, and losing his last life so that the *game over* announcement flashed across the screen. He threw his phone to the end of the bed in disgust, sulking. "I am still in love with Brynn, just as much as you are. I would die for her just as you would.

"But I don't think you would make a good husband because you haven't had as much practice. Brynn needs a male who knows what he's doing, and that takes a fair amount of practice. The kind you so sorely lack. Hard fucking practice, brother."

Bayn's eyes grew dreamy as he stared off into the distance, ignoring the jibe.

"She isn't like any other female. She is not only beautiful, but heroic. To watch her cut down Liquidators like a killing machine turns me on. When she feeds from me, I melt. She is exquisite. Her shape, her luminous eyes, the curve of her hips. I can't even imagine what the rest of her looks like."

"I'm sure she's perfect all over. If I ever had a chance to go down on her, I don't know if I would ever want to come up again," Tarren mused, his eyes focusing at a distance as he allowed himself to imagine it.

She would be perfect, pale, and silky smooth. He just knew it. He could see himself placed just between her thighs perfectly as if he were made to be there. Then his body reacted, growing long and hard. He quickly threw the comforter over his hips in one awkward jerk of movement.

Bayn's eyes widened.

He turned away and said, "I'm going downstairs. You better be there in the next five minutes, or Brynn will come up here and drag you there yourself."

Terran flushed and thought about how he wished she would come to his room just once instead of making him feed her in such a platonic area of the mansion. His muscles tensed, and his twin brother walked out the door, closing it with a slight slam behind him.

He ran his fingers through his hair, headed to his closet, and muttered, "Gods help me."

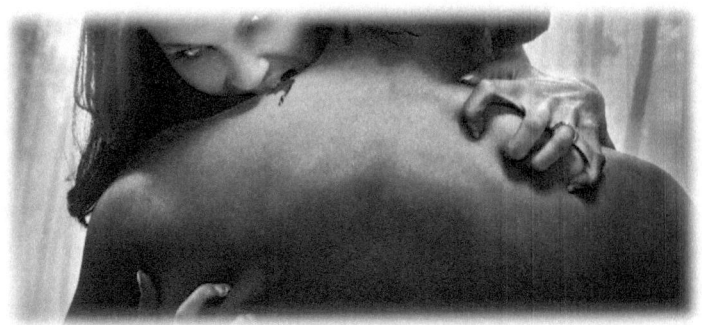

CHAPTER FIVE:
VICTORIOUS

The feast was winding down as Bayn sat stiffly in his chair. His feet were firmly planted on the floor below the long table situated within the vast dining area of the mansion. His eyes intent on Brynn as she elegantly sipped red wine from perfect stemware. Her slim body was covered in a gloriously dark fabric that clashed against her pale skin perfectly, emboldening each streak of the same shade in her hair and painted on her full lips. As he watched her, her lips curved with each syllable she spoke to the servant to her right. He could understand why his twin was equally as infatuated with her as he was. It had been this way since she came to lead the brigade. Of course, they were twins, so did that make them most likely to fall in love with the same woman? He wasn't certain. All he knew was that he couldn't tear his eyes away from her as he felt the heat flare within them.

Her crimson eyes flashed blue in the candlelight as it flickered over her face, the *Sapphire Eye* just begging to be used even though she had stored the Quaji of every Liquidator or Turncoat slain on the front lawn. He adored watching her while she did it, taking such care as she ushered them into the tiny glass jars. It was in sharp contrast to the hard coldness of her violent acts in battle.

Most of the table was deserted by now, and Bayn had chosen his seat wisely, not wanting to sit too close to Brynn as there was no telling what he would say or do. Especially since his twin had taken the quickest opportunity to sit right beside her, his eyes flaring with the same desirous heat as Bayn's. He felt Calyx's energy move around him, but he didn't say anything. He didn't even tear his eyes away from the vision at the other end of the table. The fabric of her dress reached up to cover her slender throat that produced such a velvet laugh. She sat beside him and flipped her long dark curls over her shoulder. He could see her frowning out of the corner of his eye, but he did not turn to look at her.

"You know, Bayn, if you stare too hard at her for too long you'll burn a hole in her forehead," she said jokingly, placing a comforting hand on top of his on the table.

He started a little at her touch, flushing.

"So, it's that obvious, is it?" he replied rhetorically. "Calyx, tell me honestly. Do you think Brynn would consider polyandry for the sake of us Craven twins, or will I be forced to kill Tarren to take him out of the running?"

Calyx used her napkin to squelch a smile.

"Bayn, I don't think Brynn is giving marriage any thought at all at the moment. She is more concerned with preserving the Electi and keeping our enemies at bay. I am pretty sure that she will see Gwenyth married first before she marries anyone."

"But pardon me, I happened to research Electi history. If memory serves me right, Brynn has the same option as all Summus Ducem. Whether male or female, the leader may take more than one marriage partner. And with the emphasis on breeding more of us as quickly as possible, I would like to offer the opinion that she might be in more of a hurry. We couldn't be more devoted, Calyx. As an Empath, you know that. As far as the lovely Lady Gwenyth is concerned, she needs to come out of her chambers and from behind Brynn's skirts more often. I don't see that she lacks for male attention. Just look for yourself."

Bayn gestured with his wine glass toward Gwenyth, sitting on Brynn's right side as she always was, engaged in a conversation with three eager-looking attractive males at once. Bayn bristled when he saw that one of them was Ryder, who was at that moment making Gwenyth laugh and kissing her small white hand. The *good* one that was not withered.

Gwenyth generally kept the other hand

gloved in velvet embellished with gold embroidery and seed pearls and covered her arm to just past her elbow, in her lap.

"You know I don't trust Ryder Perkins though I can't tell you why," Bayn muttered loud enough so that Calyx might hear him. "I know he has sworn fealty to the Electi, but I still think that he is a scoundrel. He probably has a wife somewhere, and a passel of brats he owes back child support on. I would never let him have my back during battle, and my brother is of the same opinion."

"Well, I trust Brynn's instincts. They can't fool her," Calyx replied. "I sense some deep wound in him. I believe he is a widower."

"What about you, Calyx?" Bayn said, turning to her inquisitively. "Is there no one seeking your favor?"

She laughed, high, throaty, and lovely.

"No, nothing like that." She waved her hand in a dismissive gesture.

"No aristocrats hoping to get into your bed? That's a shock."

Even though she was a woman of the brigade and always around males speaking in such a derogatory fashion, she blushed.

"Well, yes, but none that I would ever be interested in. They're too stuffy for my taste. I have been exposed to warriors for far too long for an aristocrat to be interesting."

Bayn nodded, turning back to look at Brynn as she continued to speak with his brother, her luscious lips curled up into a pleased smile. How badly he wanted to be kissing those lips, making her feel every ounce of pleasure his body wanted to grant her, but he couldn't. And all because of his brother's affliction with her. He had never been in such a horrid place in his life. The House had assigned him to take his place in the brigade Brynn took over. Living with her under the same roof didn't make things any easier, either. If anything, it made his ache and hunger for her even stronger and more painful. Seeing her speak so candidly with Tarren at that moment didn't help in the slightest. He began to push himself up from his chair, hands on the arms of it as he scooted backward.

"I need to go," he whispered as he turned to glance at Calyx, her green eyes glowing in the soft light.

The flickers of the candles only made them sparkle even more, causing them to nearly blaze. Suddenly, Brynn had left her chair and made her way toward them, sauntering in all of her beauty. A beauty he felt he couldn't have.

She moved quickly, placing her hand lovingly on one of his.

"Please, don't leave, Bayn. Maybe we can take a stroll. It is night now after all, and you look like you could use the company. Maybe even to talk?"

"Oh, I don't know, Brynn. I—"

She raised her hand, interjecting. "What is there to know about, Bayn? Just one leisurely stroll on the grounds. They have been deemed safe enough, and you need someone to talk to. Well," she took a step back with her hand on his arm still, her long red gown flowing behind her as she took his hand and began to make her way toward the door, "as safe as they can be for a vampire."

She laughed, and it was infectious, Bayn chuckling slightly at the small joke. Tarren was watching them warily, causing Bayn to smirk at his brother.

"Alright, let's go for a walk. Maybe the fresh air will clear my mind a little."

She smiled as she led him toward the front entrance, holes, and pockmarks on the floor from the weapons that had struck it earlier. It reminded him of the danger they had been in. The attack from the Liquidators and their Turncoat traitors was enough to make him shake his head at the betrayal, but he was confident that Calyx had felt that same betrayal even deeper. Her own Fae blood ran through the veins of the Turncoats, and he could sense the hatred within her when she encountered one. It wasn't just because she felt it. He felt it too and honestly hated it for her. He hated it when she had to kill her own for justice and the safety of the House of Electi, but what could he do? Nothing more than fight by her side and comfort her when needed. Then he would think of Brynn and her lovely scent and how badly he wanted to kiss her and make love to her in his bed. To be hers and only hers. He was pathetic.

He knew his brother Tarren would think

him pathetic too. That was the difference between them. Tarren was much more forceful in all things. He never showed his hand, but once he decided what he wanted, he would wait for exactly the right time and then zero in on it like an eagle in flight.

Tarren always seemed to get what he wanted without much of a fight.

Bayn was of a slightly more cautious nature, though equally as single-minded in his pursuits. Even though they were identical twins, Bayn was more hesitant in how he managed his wants. When they wanted the same female, he suspected that Tarren might trump him in the end.

The air outside was cool, though thick with humidity. In the soft lamplight above them, her fabulously wild hair glinted red gold and seemed to have a life of its own.

Even the curve of her back was sheer poetry.

What would Tarren do if he were in the garden with Brynn? he thought to himself. And then suddenly, as Brynn stopped to look up at the full lantern of a moon, he knew.

"What are you thinking, Brynn?" he asked quietly, daring to slip one arm loosely around her perfect waist. "Sometimes I find myself wondering. All your thoughts can't be of war and Gwenyth's welfare. Don't you have other interests? Hobbies?"

Brynn turned. In the half-light of the moon, she was more beautiful than ever, her pleasing facial planes accentuated and her ruby-hued eyes glowing under their long gold-tipped lashes that curled so elegantly.

She smirked.

"War is my hobby and my vocation," she said.

"Well, you need to get a new one," Bayn answered. "We almost lost you twice recently. It's getting tiresome, and I wouldn't say this in front of Calyx or Tarren, but I have to tell you I've noticed that you are taking more chances lately than you used to. You're getting addicted to the adrenaline rush... at least, that's what I think."

"And... what if I am?" she replied, standing toe to toe with him. "What if it's my drug of choice? What if being near death makes me feel more alive and awakens all my sleeping neurons? What if I just plain like it, Bayn? What if all there is for me is bloodshed, death, and that hum of pleasure within my body that it all brings?"

"Ah, Brynn, there are so many other things even more thrilling," Bayn told her, looking down and getting lost in her raw beauty.

Then he decided to do what Tarren would do. He went for it.

At first, when his mouth covered hers he felt a slight electrical charge, but soon he couldn't tell where his mouth ended, and hers began. For a few seconds, he was swept up in a reverie beyond pleasure. Her lips were sweet and soft, and he wanted the kiss to go on forever.

But it didn't and was over far too soon.

Brynn pulled back — her face flushed. For a single moment, she looked confused and vulnerable, shocking him because he'd never seen her exhibit either quality.

"Bayn, we can't. I must have had too much wine. You know I can drink you and Tarren under the table. This is not professional behavior. And..."

"And just for a moment you were letting yourself be a female," Bayn interrupted. "Not a bad choice, I think."

He grinned at her conspiratorially, his white teeth flashing in the darkness as his fangs throbbed with the need for her that rushed into him.

"I can't apologize for kissing you, Brynn. It may not be what you wanted, but I think it's what you needed. It means something to me that the Daughter of the Electi who yields to no one on the battlefield yielded her perfect pink lips to mine."

"Oh, just stop," Brynn said crossly, stepping on his boot-clad foot on purpose and moving past him. "If you speak of it I will have your squawking head on a platter at the next victory feast. Understand? I need to check on Gwenyth. You can either come with me or stand here gazing at the moon by yourself."

As Bayn watched, she gathered her skirts in both hands and flounced up the path back toward the sounds of music and raucous laughter. His heart was beating in pure triumph that he had succeeded in something he never thought he would.

He'd made the boldest move he'd ever made. He had kissed the most beautiful creature on the planet. Before she'd disengaged, her small tongue had danced for a few glorious, unforgettable moments with his own. It made him yearn even more for her, a hunger for so much more penetrating his very core.

She was *into* him. He was sure of it.

The next morning was a quiet one. Brynn had received word from the Surgeon that the dark-haired stranger she'd nearly killed had recovered enough so that he could be interrogated without being affected by his injuries.

She could hardly wait. Just the fact that he'd bled red was enough to intrigue her. She couldn't sense what he was, but it was neither Liquidator or Turncoat. She had to find the answer.

First, she wanted to have breakfast with Gwenyth and discuss the huge Victory Feast the night before. To that end, she had breakfast brought to her private chambers by the servants: popovers, Gwenyth's favorite since childhood, with loads of butter and jam, eggs, and a rasher of bacon. They also had a pot of chocolate and one of tea brought along with a generous bowl of clotted cream. And, of course, two full crystal tumblers of fresh human blood from the donors. They could be sustained by human blood, some Electi living off of it their entire lives, but when it came to a grave injury or a quick boost of energy only, another member of their race would do.

"Yum," Gwenyth remarked, biting into a heavily laden popover. "It's been forever since we had a leisurely breakfast together. This is fun, Brynn."

Brynn stopped crunching on a strip of bacon and leaned over to pat Gwenyth's knee.

"I am sorry. I've neglected you. I had been planning a picnic before the mansion was attacked. It seems as though the attacks are escalating. I do wish we could spend more time together. Ride horses, picnic, or even go shopping or something."

"Shopping," Gwenyth replied, though her mouth was so full that it came out *thopping*. "We need new clothing. Brynn, you haven't bought anything in ages, and I know we aren't poor. We had all those artifacts that were our parents when we left Uncle Vincent. They couldn't possibly be all gone now, and we need to blend in with the humans. We can't stay locked up forever."

"Far from all gone," Brynn answered. "But selling the artifacts is a tricky business. It is a very exclusive market. One for billionaires with the taste for the precious and unusual and the means to satisfy that taste. It's not like going to the bank. It can take months to find the right buyer for a piece. Plus, it costs me an incredible amount of money to provide for our Guard and soldiers. But no worries. We have plenty of items to sell and quite a bit of money in the bank just now. Of course, we can go shopping."

Gwenyth leaned forward as if she'd just thought of something.

"Do we still have the Red Star?" she asked. "You haven't had to sell it, Brynn, have you?"

"No, my darling," Brynn assured her. "That is yours. I would never sell it. Mother always meant for you to have it, just like she always meant for me to have the Blue Star. We were to wear them on our wedding days but Gwen, if you would like to wear it today, you can. I don't see the use of such a beautiful piece sitting in my vault for years. You should wear it today. It matches your eyes exquisitely."

"And, sister, while I am excited to be able to wear it, what do you mean by 'sitting in my vault for years?'" Gwen stated, doing her best finger quotes around the words her older sister had said exactly. "Are you trying to say I will never find a male that I will marry? One that will love me as I deserve? Am I not worthy of that?"

She stood and took a few steps away from her sister, practically fuming and clenching her fists in anger.

"No, Gwenyth, that's not what I'm saying. I would never. You deserve all the happiness in the world. You know I believe that, so where is this coming from?"

Brynn set the crispy strip of bacon down on the plate in front of her, watching Gwenyth's back as she attempted to compose herself. Brynn had always protected her as best she could, and she couldn't understand the drastic change in her sister's mood as they spoke.

"Just forget it, Brynn. You cannot protect me forever, even from your own thoughts. Let's just forget about the conversation, go shopping for something that you can go out into the city in, and try to enjoy ourselves, huh? Let's just be us for a little while."

With those words she stormed out of the room, slamming the door behind her.

Brynn wasn't sure what to think about her sister's outburst. She wasn't known to be extremely emotional for any reason, even if it was well-founded. She sighed and picked up the piece of bacon again, crunching on it as she stared at the door and wondered why she couldn't just keep her mouth shut sometimes.

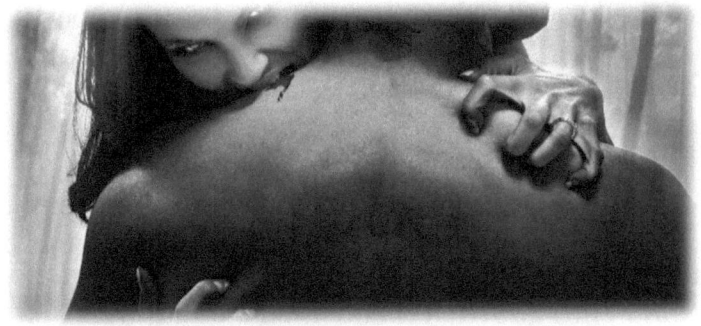

CHAPTER SIX:
THE PRICE OF MISCHIEF

Trace and Jupiter, known as *Jupe*, were best friends and had gone through the rigors of Warrior Training together since early childhood. They both felt important and a bit superior to the other twenty or so students in the Stealth Class because they had turned twelve only fourteen days apart, a critical age for those serving under the Daughter of the Electi.

They knew their Initiation would be soon, and then they would be seen fit to join in the frequent battles. It was the greatest rite of passage for a young warrior, and each young soldier coming of age was assigned a member of the Royal Guard to be their Guardian. They would continue to learn and grow under their guidance.

Trace and Jupe, having shown early promise, had been chosen by the Craven twins who would serve as their mentors. The boys

61

felt superior to their classmates because both Tarren and Bayn were idolized like rock stars for their prowess in battle and their embodiment of the finest male attributes of their race. Both the youths aspired to become skilled warriors and protectors just like them.

Perhaps soon they would be able to fight alongside the twins. As one of the Ortis or *rising* elite guard, Trace was assigned to Tarren and Jupe to Bayn. The bonds formed between guardians and their young protégés were considered among the most sacred and permanent in the culture of the Electi, never-ending even in death.

One of the primary purposes of the training was to instill toughness and stealth in the youth. To this end, they were trained rigorously in acrobatic warfare, sword and knife play, and wall climbing with an emphasis on upper body strength and endurance.

This particular day, as the class participants stood barefoot on the Alchemy circular symbols spaced at precise distances apart on the stone floor of their airy classroom, Trace's practical joker streak kicked in as Natalia, regal as ever and not missing a step though totally blind, entered the front of the classroom.

All the students automatically bowed in deference, shouting, "Oracle" in tribute to her.

This was customary when addressing their teacher and all other elders within their race. It had been ingrained in them since they were able to understand the action.

Natalia began as she usually did, with a lecture on the merits of Stealth Training and a historical retrospective of battles in which the stealth of the Guard had contributed in some grand way to the victory that was guaranteed to come to them as long as they held to these merits.

There were strict rules concerning classroom behavior with no horseplay or eating in class allowed, but as Natalia continued speaking, Trace, who had arrived late to breakfast, removed a bunch of grapes from the pocket of his gym shorts. He crammed a few in his mouth and then held them up so that Jupe could see them.

Jupe held out his hand, and when Trace threw him a grape, another student saw it and hissed at him to throw one to him as well.

As more and more of the gathered students became aware of the game, they held their hands out to catch the grapes Trace dispersed. His face flushed with excitement, Trace lobbed more grapes at eager classmates, barely stifling a laugh when one of the most athletic of them jumped straight up and caught the grape in his mouth.

He was having an excellent time. Part of his enjoyment was putting one over on Natalia. Although he had respect for her, after all, she was an Oracle *yadayadayada*, he wasn't in the mood for a lecture. It amused him to take advantage of her lack of sight. His classmates were certainly enjoying the joke.

Then one of the girls up front, her dark braided hair wrapped around her head, motioned to him. Trace tossed a grape her way, but she missed catching it, and it plopped to the floor rolling in front of Natalia, who often paced back and forth as she lectured. It rolled under her sandal just as she stepped forward.

The squishing sound it made seemed to echo in the chamber, sounding like it was on a sound system. Natalia stopped short, and Jupe threw his best friend a look of horror. Natalia reached down and removed her sandal from her slender foot, her glazed-over eyes unfocused as they flicked over the room.

"Trace Vexo, will you please come to the front of the class," she said, the tone of her cultured voice echoing against the walls.

Gulping, his heart beating loudly in his chest, Trace walked to the front of the classroom. It seemed like a long walk. With her eyes glazed over by the opalescent film that Oracles always had, Natalia seemed more formidable close-up and somewhat frightening as he approached her.

"What do you have to say for yourself, future Guardian?" she asked.

Trace found himself tongue-tied as he scrambled for his next words.

"I apologize, Oracle," he said, hanging his head. "I meant no disrespect."

At this Natalia threw back her head and laughed, startling him, and causing his head to jerk up in surprise.

"That is as preposterous a statement as I have ever heard uttered within these walls. You are too close to the end of your training for childish acts. Certainly, there is a time and a place for frivolity and mirth, but not inside these walls. These walls contain the future of the Electi. It is a serious business to show disregard for the knowledge that assures our survival. Do you understand?"

"Yes, Oracle" Trace replied.

The classroom had gone deadly silent, and he wished fervently for the stone floor to open up and swallow him whole instead of being forced to face the embarrassment of Natalia's lecture.

"You have no idea that although my eyes are useless, I see more clearly than any of you," the Oracle mused. "My blindness is a gift that allows me to see not only this world, but beyond it. I saw what you were doing from the beginning. I could sense the change in your breathing, hear your whispers and the change in air currents talked to me and told me exactly what you were doing. Still, I waited, hoping that your wisdom might override your foolishness and when I called you up here I felt your sphincter tighten, and your balls shrivel up in fear. That is how well I see you. You may return to your place, Trace Vexo."

Trace stared at Natalia, surprised.

"Am I not to be punished?" he said aloud.

"Of course, you will have a consequence," Natalia told him, the film over her eyes seeming to glow. "It will be exacted on your Guardian, Tarren. As your Guardian, he has taken it upon himself to bear the brunt of your indiscretions, and you will get to watch."

Gwenyth was irate with her older sister, but she wanted to spend alone time with her. Even if it meant getting dressed in clothes she didn't understand, wearing a glove without the dazzle she was accustomed to, and being surrounded by loud and boisterous human beings.

They had been chauffeured to the Del Almo Mall and rode in silence, Gwenyth not being able to even look at Brynn. She may have overreacted to her sister's suggestion of being able to wear the trinket her mother had left her, but she didn't want to be a burden to her. Brynn was always protecting her from the whispers of others, but she wanted to be able to speak for herself without her big sister coming to her rescue.

Gwenyth had to admit that her outburst was not entirely Brynn's fault. She had felt, for the first time, dissatisfaction with their Electi lifestyle. Her role in particular. It seemed as if her entire life other people had been making her decisions for her. First, it was their mother and father. Then their Uncle Vincent, and finally her older sister Brynn.

That had been all fine and good when she was a child, but she wasn't a child anymore.

She found herself smothered by the virtual cotton wool wrapping of her sister's overprotective ways. However well-intentioned, she couldn't continue to play along with it. Brynn would probably be surprised and alarmed at Gwenyth's thoughts. Her priorities had shifted, and she wanted different things than she had before.

She wanted to train in Warfare skills under the Craven twins. The thrill of the battle was in her blood just as surely as it flowed in Brynn's, and she could no longer deny that part of herself.

She also wanted more freedom in her relationships. She wanted to pick her companions without running everything by Brynn. Brynn was too quick to dismiss Gwenyth's subtle hints about spending more time with members of the Guard or members of the School of Warfare. Every time Gwenyth brought up the name of someone she'd like to get to know better, Brynn would shut her down by reminding her that she was a highborn Daughter of the Electi and as such could not associate with those beneath her station.

Well, that was bullshit. Gwenyth knew Brynn hadn't been much older than she was now when she organized her army and began fighting Liquidators.

Gwenyth settled back in the seat, a smile briefly crossing her lips.

It was her secret that she had made a

special connection the other night. Brynn hadn't been around when it had happened because she had elected to take a stroll with Bayn. As soon as Brynn had left, Ryder Perkins had taken a seat next to her, kissing her right hand and repeating the oath of fealty that was the customary greeting.

Gwenyth was flattered. She didn't know exactly how old Ryder was, but she knew he was older. Up close, he was even more handsome with dark hair to his shoulders, a closely cropped beard, and dark brows framing his surprisingly blue eyes. He asked after her and then launched into a genuine and natural conversation, querying her about what her hobbies were as well as her aspirations. His interest in her seemed natural and authentic, and even though Tarren, sitting a few seats away, glared at Ryder the entire time, Ryder took it in stride.

Just before Brynn returned, as though he could feel that his time in Gwenyth's company was running out, he squeezed her leg above her knee and pressed something into her hand.

"For you, Gwenyth, Daughter of the Electi," he had said. "The loveliest lady here, and the smartest despite your youth. This is a keepsake, and I ask that you wear it and think of me. If you do, I know I will be kept safe to return to you."

He disappeared from her side in an instant, but she could still feel the warmth on her knee where his large hand rested. Just his touch seemed to awaken her as though from a spell.

She'd looked up and saw Brynn was moving closer, obviously ticked off at Bayn for something as she usually was. She managed to steal a glance at the curious object in her hand.

It was a small, hammered medallion on a thin long silver chain. It had a single letter engraved in fancy scrollwork on the front of it.

It was the letter R.

She'd hidden it in her pocket and waited until later, when she'd finally been completely alone, to fasten it around her neck. Because she was so small-boned, it was virtually undetectable beneath her clothing and the tiny round medallion hung well below her small breasts.

She had no desire to wear the family jewelry that was her legacy. The Star necklace was just for show and meant nothing.

Ryder's gift, however, was to her young mind a secret promise.

That was the necklace she would wear.

Hours after their stressful meal, Brynn and a sullen Gwenyth came back with bags upon bags of clothing swathed by the full moon. Now they sat in the front row to watch the ceremony that would take place in the underground tunnels of the Warrior Training Academy.

It was a ceremony to be performed with all seriousness in accordance with time-honored ritual and attended by every young Warrior in Training that resided there. But it would not be followed by a celebration.

It was a rare ceremony not held in over half a century, and it was based on the Laws of the Electi recognizing the sacred connection between young Warriors and their Mentors. It reasoned that, due to the seriousness of the bond between them both, the transgressions of either the Mentor or his charge should be dealt with in a prescribed manner.

The ceremony was called the *Igitur*, the *Consequence*, and Natalia was in charge of deciding exactly what the consequence would be for Trace Vexo's misbehavior in class. The ceremony was held in the Room of Fountains, an inner sanctum of the Warfare School that was oval-shaped. The curving inner wall of the room held several niche fountains, each depicting a fallen Warrior of the Electi. During award celebrations, the fountains were lit with brightly colored lights and enhanced with music.

For the *Igitur*, the fountains ran gray and silent, their carved stonework standing in what seemed silent reproach for Trace's misdeed. Trace hadn't taken his training seriously until Tarren, the massive Electi Warrior, was granted Guardianship over him. Because of this, he would face the consequences of that burden. Trace watched in silence as the sanctum doors opened. The

70

Daughters of Electi were the first to enter after Natalia had prepared both Tarren and Trace for what was to come.

The sanctum was filled with students, teachers, and Electi Warriors, all standing solemnly and wearing their formal attire. That included gray capes lined with blood-red silk and embroidered in silver thread on the back with the insignia of the school. The image of the sun's rays surrounded a Phoenix rising from the ashes adorned each cape as well as the wall behind the podium where Tarren would face his duty head-on.

On the raised twelve-inch by twelve-inch podium in the center, Trace stood to face Tarren, his Sworn Guardian and Mentor. Natalia's face was covered by the shadow of the hood of her long ceremonial cape. She walked around the two as she began speaking, taking each step slowly as if she walked too quickly she may stumble.

"We are gathered this evening to restore balance," she began, her powerful voice echoing off the stone surrounding them. "Youth can never be an excuse for failing to uphold the standards of the Warring Arts School. Depending on circumstance, any of you could be called upon to die for our kind. One of the fountains in this sacred place was dedicated to a fallen hero who gave his life battling Liquidators who attempted to storm the Estate soon after we first arrived. He was the first to meet the sword of the encroaching Liquidators and gave the alarm so that others might be saved. His name was Tempest Ryan, and he was nine years old."

Reverent silence stole the room for all of a moment.

"There is no place for horseplay during our training sessions. You will need every bit of instruction we can impart, internalizing it and absorbing it. The student here who is the subject of the Igitur Ceremony shall be nameless and invisible for the next four weeks. Any student seen conversing with him will face his own Igitur and their Guardian will be punished."

Natalia whipped around suddenly and addressed Tarren, who stood silent and as immobile as if made of stone.

"Do you understand why you are being punished this evening?" she asked.

"Yes, Oracle," was the only answer Tarren made as he and Trace faced each other.

Trace stood silently, but inwardly he was experiencing the kind of torture that only those who have caused hurt to those they love and admire the most ever experience. He could only guess at the disappointment Tarren must feel, and he had regretted his actions ever since he disrespected the charge of a rising Electi Warrior.

Now Tarren would be punished in his stead, basically for trusting and believing in him and taking an oath to stand with him, even if it meant taking on his punishments as his own.

He would have rather been whipped himself, Trace thought in silent agony. Of course, Natalia was right. The greater lesson would be having to witness Tarren punished in his place. He searched Tarren's eyes frantically as he stood opposite him. It would have been a relief to see reproach in them or hatred, but whatever Tarren's thoughts, whatever his disappointment, nothing in his manner gave evidence of it.

A gong sounded. Tarren dropped the cloak he wore and stood bare-chested and barebacked, his torso exposed to the chill that had descended on the chamber. Trace watched as goose bumps broke out over the male's bronze flesh, quickly disappearing as his body adjusted to the temperature of the room.

From out of nowhere, Natalia produced a Rahaz-Estar Bane whip. One of the most elegant and deadliest weapons known to be used by the Electi and never once in battle. Tarren dropped to his knees before her in reverence and duty, his back turned to the Oracle. Very quickly, she administered lashes to Tarren's exposed back, cutting diamond-shaped patterns in his exposed skin as each lash rang out and echoed within the sanctum. Tarren never once screamed or cried out, his face remaining stoic as he took the beating, his eyes closed and lips tight in a straight line.

Natalia was an expert. She had the strength to administer blows that could slice flesh to the bone, but she held back, wanting only to deliver enough punishment to cure Trace of his foolish and immature behavior.

As he watched Tarren accept the punishment that should have been his without flinching, Trace was unable to keep tears of shame from running down his face. Dark spots littered the inside of his cape just below his chin, his tears marking it for all to see so they could also bear witness to his foolishness.

When Natalia finished the whipping, the Bane Whip disappeared up into Natalia's voluminous sleeve again. She took a step away from Tarren's exposed and bleeding back.

"It is finished," she said.

All present filed out silently except for Brynn who watched Trace and Tarren warily, coming to kneel before Tarren who had not moved once since the lashings ended. As soon as the room was empty except for the four of them, Tarren replaced his cloak, wincing as he did so with Brynn's helping hand. When the warrior stood, Trace ran to him, collapsing against his broad and sweaty chest, sobbing uncontrollably.

"Never," he sobbed. "Never again, I swear."

Natalia left the chamber without a word, and Trace's fervent cries echoed up the tunnel and reached her exceptionally keen ears. She smiled grimly.

Though it would not be for some time, she had seen a vision as she whipped Tarren. She had foreknowledge of something neither

Tarren nor Trace had any inkling of.

Despite the bonding, love, and trust between them, an unforeseen betrayal was in store. And it would rock the House of Electi to its very foundation.

Tarren couldn't help but think about the rough week that was now behind him. His charge, his little Soul Brother Trace, had managed to offend Natalia — one of the most powerful beings serving the Electi. She was also one of the most powerful weapons against the Liquidators and the Fae traitors.

After showering gingerly the evening of the Ignitus Ceremony, he had surveyed the damages. His back had been lashed in a repeating diamond pattern by her whip, the marks already beginning to scab over. Typically, at the hand of another being wielding any other weapon, his wounds would have been completely healed in mere minutes. But Natalia's whip was enchanted. Tarren would bear the scars from the wounds she had inflicted for six months or more and, if he were lucky, he would be able to feed to help speed the process. Hopefully, that would spare him two months of recovery.

At least, he was confident Trace had gotten the message. Tarren admired the youth from the start, and hand-picked him so the lessons he had learned in training would not be lost. Brash, thoughtlessly brave, and arrogant. Trace reminded Tarren of a younger version of himself. For that reason alone, he loved him. Loved his fierceness, his determination to excel, and even his snarkiness.

Last night had been an epiphany for them both. Tarren partly blamed himself for Trace's behavior. Tarren knew that he had neglected to spend the necessary time with the youth, and he felt guilty as a result. Frequent Liquidator and Rogue attacks had taken up most of his time lately, but the neglect of his charge would have to change if there was any hope for the youngster.

Even so, he knew that Natalia had judged wisely and meted out the punishment in the measure in which it was needed. Trace was still fearless — the slicing blows had crushed only his arrogance, irreverence, and obstinance.

They were so deeply connected on the spiritual level that they did not need to exchange any words after the Ignitus. The shared experience had been equally painful for them both, and Tarren was confident that his physical agony would teach the boy a lesson.

Now they shared shame, perhaps more potent than shared glory. It deepened their connection, and it was up to him to engrave it into their very souls just as it should be.

CHAPTER SEVEN:
CREED

"**Y**ou look incredible in that bikini," Gwenyth complained loudly.

Her arms were folded over her chest as she surveyed Brynn's flawless pink and white flesh, her private parts barely concealed by the scant and flimsy material of the hot pink two-piece bathing suit she wore.

"It's so unfair that you got mother's boobs. I am practically flat-chested. That completely sucks."

Brynn chuckled as she surveyed herself in the three-way dressing room mirror of her massive closet. She had taken her shades off and thrown them onto the bureau, the vibrant pink color striking with her ruby eyes.

"I do thank Mom, but I have to tell you having these breasts is very inconvenient in battle. I have to strap them down to protect them sometimes, and our enemy doesn't take a woman in combat seriously. Anyway," she continued, "You aren't finished growing. When I was your age, I was 34B too. You will be amazed at the changes coming."

A knock outside of the massive closet interrupted Brynn, her head snapping toward the sound. Bayn stood just within the threshold. His eyes studied her with a lust he attempted to hide, but failed epically. The look in his eyes made Brynn think of the kiss in the garden during the Victory dinner. Heat crept up into her cheeks, and she turned back to the mirror, hoping he hadn't seen it.

"Yes, Bayn. What is it? Hopefully, that prisoner of ours survived and is ready for interrogation," she quipped, sincerely hoping he had survived his injuries.

She loved to administer an interrogation because, if they didn't open up, she could make them and no one would say a word. All because of what he was or what they thought he was. She was still perplexed by the color of his blood.

"Yes, he is much recovered," Bayn agreed, searching her eyes for any recognition of what had transpired between them and finding none. "Surprisingly so. You should be careful. Even the Surgeon is not sure what manner of miscreant we are dealing with."

Brynn stripped off the bikini and let it fall to the floor, gathering the clothes she had worn out to the mall. That was when she heard the breath catch in Bayn's chest, audible and oh-so-obvious. She had never once cared who saw her sacred flesh, but she was beginning to wonder if she should take more care around the twin. He had an all too apparent infatuation with her that she wasn't even certain she wanted to explore.

"Fine," Brynn answered brusquely.

Inwardly, she was irritated beyond reason at the love-struck puppy dog look on Bayn's face, so much so that she wanted to slap him and yell, "Snap out of it!"

It had been a kiss. A drunken one. Nothing more. At least, not to her. What was that expression among the Electi? "Wine sweetens the lips and warms the valley of desire, but come the morn you have lain with a Liar?" Or something like that. She wasn't about to neither encourage a repeat performance nor give him the idea he had impressed her. She was all business and expected no less from him.

Once fully dressed, she brushed past him and strode down the corridor, her boots loudly echoing on the natural stone tile floors. Bayn's heavier steps sounded behind her, and beyond that, it seemed as if a third set also followed.

Brynn turned around, fixing Gwenyth with a steely gaze.

"No. Absolutely, not. You are not coming to the cells with us, Gwenyth. Now go back to your room."

Brynn had to give Gwenyth credit. She staunchly stood her ground and glared back, a smaller version of her intimidating older sister right down to the defiant expression on her lovely face.

"I'm not a child," she said, "and if we are currently training twelve-year-old boys to fight against the Liquidators and die, then you are way past time to teach your sister how to protect herself. Oh, you've done a dandy job of keeping me safe. You've kept me so safe that I wouldn't know a Liquidator if it sat on my face and wiggled."

Despite trying not to, Bayn snorted and bent his head as if he were smoothing his hair so Brynn wouldn't see his amused expression.

Brynn sighed with frustration. She always knew this day would come, though she dreaded it. She had an answer at the ready.

"Then come if you want, but I warn you. What you see won't be pretty, or smell lovely. If you have night terrors, you will only have yourself to blame, dear sister. But yes, come along. I think you should. It will at least cure you of your foolish curiosity."

As soon as Brynn had turned and was walking again, Bayn and Gwenyth smiled at each other and silently fist-bumped behind her back. It wasn't often Brynn acquiesced to someone else's suggestion, particularly in matters having to do with Liquidators.

If that was truly what this imprisoned creature was.

As the hidden elevator at the end of the hallway descended five floors to a sub-basement area, Gwenyth's stomach lurched and her early triumph turned to anxiety. What if Brynn was right? What if the very appearance of the Liquidator, or whatever he was, gave her nightmares?

Her DNA-based bravado took effect, and she squared her slight shoulders. She would not wimp out by showing fear or even disgust. She would take her cues from Brynn and follow her lead. After all, if the Daughters of the Electi did not show courage, they could not expect their followers to be fearless, could they?

When they reached the bottommost floor, the old elevator creaked open. Brynn immediately addressed the five members of the guard stationed in front of the main gate to the cells. All of them saluted as soon as they saw Brynn and then dropped to one knee.

"At ease," she said.

Both guards rose from their position on the floor and listened intently to their leader.

"I need a more recent update. Is the prisoner talking? Eating? Does he piss and shit? What manner of creature do you find him to be?"

The General Surgeon stepped forward and regarded the Daughter of Electi with a curt nod.

"He does not speak, although one of the guards heard him singing. His blood is red, not black, though a deeper hue than ours. He heals nearly like a vampire, though slightly slower. I am doing some genetic testing on his blood. He is unusually strong. We have had to keep him shackled with the enchanted chains and fetters as a precaution because of his tremendous strength."

Brynn nodded, rolling the information the surgeon just gave her over in her mind, still unsure of what to make of any of it.

"Excellent. Take me to him," she ordered.

When Brynn and her entourage found themselves in front of one of the larger cells, she was startled by the appearance of the muscular humanoid shackled against the far wall. The cell was clean and sterile with white walls and shining iron bars. His tanned flesh was even starker against the brightness of it. She had expected dirty, ugly, and glowering as he knelt before her.

What she saw before her looked like a modern-day gladiator with dark hair that hung in random loose curls to his collar bones and a five 'o'clock shadow. His dark brows arched intelligently over wide-set dark eyes of indeterminate color. He had a straight nose and lips that were laterally generous. If that wasn't disconcerting enough, he had a goddamn superhero cleft in his chin that made Brynn sigh. She had always been a sucker for a cleft chin, and she had to kick herself mentally to stop from removing the shackles right then and there and taking him as a woman should.

Her voice did not belie her emotions as she had the guard unlock the cell and stepped in between the iron bars, the stranger watching her intently as if he were curious rather than fearful.

She looked down at him and said in a haughty tone, "Stand, Liquidator. You are in the presence of a Daughter of Electi."

The captive hesitated just enough to make her ire rise. If he had hesitated a nanosecond longer, she would have enjoyed lopping off his head and displaying it that evening for all to see to know that she would not be seen playing games with those who stood against them.

"Daughter of the Electi," he said, giving a slight nod while still holding her gaze. "So, this is who I was fighting. So small, you are. Yet you fought so fiercely I thought that there was more than one of you trying to kill me."

He said all of this with a smirk as if doubting her fierceness would get a rise out of her. He was attempting to incite a tantrum, but also showed he admired her strength.

Brynn ignored the captive's attempt at a backhanded compliment.

"What are you?" she asked, stepping close enough to him that she could catch the scent coming off him.

Yet another thing she attempted to ignore. He smelled like musk and the darkly delicious scent of the soap they cleaned prisoners with. It was in no way extravagant, but the smell of his maleness underneath it made it nearly tempting to touch him. He was dressed only in a roughhewn pair of shorts that trailed down long enough to cover his upper thighs, long-boned and muscular. He was tall — very tall — perhaps taller than

Bayn and Tarren, which was astonishing in itself.

"With all due respect, why should I tell you anything?" he countered. "Is this how the Electi conduct torture sessions? With a 'Q-and-A'? Why not just get to the point? Bring out the Spanish Donkey, or the Sicilian Bull, the Judas Cradle, the Iron Maiden, the lead sprinkler? Am I missing anything? Isn't that the way you medieval throwbacks do things?"

Brynn gave him a brittle smile and took another step toward him, crossing her arms over her chest. Bayn made a move to stay in line with her. She shot him a look of blatant disapproval, so he stopped himself.

"I see that your inept leaders epically misinformed you. We have everything you can imagine, including state-of-the-art *chemical persuaders*, if you will. We don't need to torture those who are reckless enough to become our captives. We usually just dispose of them. I do, however, own some torture artifacts, including a pair of sterling silver crocodile shears that I am immensely fond of and am dying to use again."

When he didn't react, she tapped one elegant boot on the floor and tossed her hair back.

"What's your name? You're boring me already, and when I'm bored, I kill things."

"Really?" the captive answered in a mild tone. "So do I. We seem to have a lot in common. Who would have guessed?"

Brynn was so intent on grilling the

stranger, she did not hear Gwenyth come up from behind her until she heard her take in a breath, staring at the stranger with rapt fascination plain on her face.

"Just kill him, Brynn," she said, her eyes sparkling. "I think I know exactly who this is." She took a few brazen steps into the cell, stopping just shy of Brynn's back. "I read about him. He is the estranged half-blood son of King Uictore, the leader of the Liquidators. His name is..."

"Creed," the stranger said, cutting Gwenyth off mid-sentence. "Pleased to make your acquaintance, Daughter of the Electi, even though you suggested my death just a moment ago. You're so bloodthirsty for someone so young."

Brynn glanced back at her sister, taking in the anticipation evident in the set of her mouth.

"And you said you needed to train at the school, huh? I don't believe you even need it."

Brynn heard the scraping sound of a heavy metal short sword being pulled from a scabbard and realized for the first time that Gwenyth had armed herself. Gwenyth brandished the sword and sent Brynn a pleading look.

"Please, let me kill him, sister. He called me *young*."

Brynn was both pleased and amused by Gwenyth's response, but her demeanor didn't reveal her intense amusement at her little sister's reaction. She was attempting to remain the cold leader she had made certain every Liquidator knew of, and she was not about to waver.

"I promise that if I decide to have him killed today he is yours, dear sister," she responded. "For now, he is mine."

The sound of heavy boots approaching the cell was heard, and Tarren appeared in the cell opening. Brynn raised her eyebrows in surprise. She'd purposely not included Tarren, reasoning that he might still be recovering from his wounds from the Ignitus Ceremony. He looked fit as a fiddle already. Or he was at least putting on a brave face because he knew the prisoner was within their walls.

He gave her a brief nod with one eyebrow raised as if to say, *You should know better than to try and leave me behind.*

"Hail, Daughter of the Electi. I am at your service," he said.

Creed, the captive, seemed amused at Tarren's appearance.

"I see you hire retired Chippendale's dancers for your bodyguards. I should like to see them dance sometime."

The words were barely out of his mouth when Tarren rushed past the trio in front of him and delivered a powerful blow to the prisoner's midsection that caused him to double over, coughing and gasping for air immediately. Tarren returned to his position with a self-satisfied look on his face.

"If you want to continue your impertinence to a Daughter of the Electi, feel free. I could use some sparring practice, you reprobate," he stated through gritted teeth.

When Creed had managed to catch his breath, he returned, "So brave to punch a shackled man. I shall take my time with your death Tarren Craven. Yes, I know who you are. You and your brother Bayn are famous as thugs for the Electi."

There was no hiding their surprise at Creed's knowledge of the ranks of the Electi, but Brynn chose to remain calm. Tarren started forward again, but Brynn placed a staying hand on his chest.

Reaching into her pocket, she removed what appeared to be a long thin Karyx wand she had gotten from Natalia years ago when she was appointed leader. There were only two left in the world, and it had the mindfucking power to cause whoever it was directed toward to experience their darkest, deepest fears. It didn't matter how hard they fought the images displayed to them. She held it out in front of her so Creed could see it and, for the first time, she saw fear in his eyes.

"The interrogation will begin now," she muttered, placing her hand on her hip, and sauntering over to Creed to stop directly in front of him.

She twirled the Karyx wand between her delicate fingers, watching him intently as sweat broke out across his forehead and bare chest with anxiety.

Brynn turned to look at Gwenyth and said, "You shouldn't be inside the cell while this takes place. I cannot risk his aggression on you."

Gwyneth shook her head. Brynn raised a hand to motion toward the brothers. Without her notice, Bayn took her by the shoulders and led her from the cell as Terran took his place just inside the threshold.

"No, I want to be in there. I will not just stand out here and watch," Gwenyth insisted, taking her older sister's safety into account even though she had been previously frustrated with her.

"But you will," Brynn shouted sternly.

Bayn's eyes were full of apology as he closed the cell door and had the remaining guards on the outside lock the iron bars, locking Terran, himself, and Brynn inside with the massive man.

Brynn turned back to look at Creed, his stare intent on her as she stood before him. He did not look away even once. She smirked.

"Now, tell us about your mother."

Creed shook his head.

"I will not, Daughter of Electi. I don't care what you do to me, but I will not betray my mother to your ilk," Creed spat.

"Oh, you won't? We will see about that."

She flicked the Karyx wand, giving him only a small taste of what it was capable of. She saw the air just before him shudder and twinkle, an image almost taking shape before him. She could not make it out but, from his reaction, she knew he was acutely aware of what the wand would show him. Would show them. His weakness was just underneath the surface waiting to be brought into the light by the Karyx wand she held in her hand.

"Now, you do not have to tell us about her. Just her name. That's all I want," Brynn admitted.

"What will her name do for you? Nothing." He shook his head again. "It will give you nothing."

"That is none of your concern," Brynn replied as she flicked the wand again, the image flashing in the air just before him even though he had turned away from it.

It followed his gaze, making certain he would see his worst fear would become reality. He squeezed his eyes shut, bending to her torture way too easily from the looks of it. She decided to use that and do the only thing she knew to do.

She took a step toward Creed, Bayn, and Terran both taking her arms in their heavy hands to hold her back in a show of protectiveness.

"Let go of me. He will not harm me. Not if he wants to make it out of here alive."

"But Brynn—" Bayn began.

"Enough," she interjected, dismissively waving her hand. "If you cannot do as ordered, I will make you watch from the sidelines as well."

Creed began to laugh then, his melodic voice becoming even more so as it caressed her flesh and played with her heart strings. She refused to let it get to her, but then he spoke. The amusement in his voice changed her reaction toward him altogether.

"That's right, monkey. Dance for the Daughter of Electi. You make a fine pet," Creed instigated, his laugh only growing louder and more pronounced, showing just how amused he was by the fact that such a large vampire of his line bowed to the whim of a female.

"You fucki—" Bayn said as he took a step toward the prisoner.

Brynn placed a hand on his chest with just enough pressure to stop his advance, and turned back to Creed. She had to keep the situation under control.

"Quiet. All of you. Take a step back. I'll take care of him."

In that instant, she knew exactly what was necessary. She placed the tip of the Karyx wand on his bare flesh just over his heart and looked up at him with a sly grin on her face. This way he could not avoid what terrified him because it would be forced into his mind with no way to stop it unless she removed the thing from his skin. Even though his face twisted into a mixture of terror and agony, he held strong and didn't give anything up. So maybe what she was trying just wasn't enough to break the male.

She sighed, backed away, and placed the Karyx wand back where she had removed it from.

"Normally this works." She turned to the twins who were now at her back. "I have an idea."

Brynn had to hand it to the half-breed. He was made out of even stronger stuff than she had realized. Despite the terror he had shown at the appearance of the Karyx wand, he had not wavered under the stress of his ultimate fear. So she knew she would have to push him even harder. If the mental torture did not break him, then physical would have to do. She wanted to steer clear of all that until she was certain she couldn't force the information out of him without an even more brutal weapon in her hands.

From the look of him, it was going to take extreme brute force to get the information they wanted. Even if it was only a name. A name held a lot more power than most realized. She hoped that, if they could gain the information from him, this name would bring the Liquidators to their knees.

Again, she placed the wand on his skin, this time against his neck. His eyes, which had been so focused on her the entire time, began to stare off into the distance. A look of absolute horror appeared on his face as he reached outward at something unseen and shouted hoarsely.

"Mariel. No. Get away from her," he cried, swatting at the air, his voice filled with anguish.

Brynn was delighted.

"We may have our answer, gentlemen," she threw a look back over her shoulder at the twins.

A quiet voice came from outside the cell. It was Natalia, her face all but obscured by the hood of her velvet cloak.

"No," she murmured. "That was his sister, but you're getting closer. Keep up the pressure, Daughter of the Electi."

Brynn was about to reply when she felt something around her ankle. Somehow, the shackled brute against the wall had managed to get hold of her boot, trying to pull her down.

Even with all the torture she had inflicted, his eyes gleamed defiantly up at her beneath the tangle of hair over his brow.

There was a gasp all around. No one was allowed to touch a Daughter of the Electi without permission for any reason. To Brynn, it was an affront to the highest order, as well as a mocking challenge she had to answer swiftly.

She threw the wand to the side. Bayn caught it deftly in mid-air as Brynn quickly twisted her entire body in a vertical spin in one direction and then the other, forcing Creed to lose his grip. Once loose, she was furious as she spun again, kicking him in the head. Then she backed away a short distance only to attack again, a somersault that ended with a concise kick between the captive's legs.

All of the guards cringed at her move, instinctively placing protective hands over their own privates while Bayn and Tarren shifted their weight and grimaced.

The captive doubled over on his side.

"That will teach you never to touch a Daughter of the Electi," Brynn spat at him, swinging up with her foot just once more to catch him under the chin. The kick sent him backward and into the wall behind him, his back hitting the cement with a distinct slap. She stalked toward him and kneeled before him, wiping her hands clean on her pants even though they were soiled with her sweat as well as her captive's from being in such proximity to him during his torture.

"Brynn, do you think it wise to get so close?" Terran asked as he took just one step forward, worry flickering across his face.

"Now Terran, he wouldn't dream of touching me again. Would you?" she asked Creed in a mocking tone.

He breathed heavily, his eyes flicking up to stare at her. A smirk crossed his lips that she hadn't expected. Her breath caught in her throat at the sensuality contained in his expression. His hair hung over his eyes, but she saw the smoldering heat inside them as it peeked out at her under thick lashes. Brynn's heart fluttered in her chest at the sight, but she held the air of superiority as she stared at him, her crimson eyes never once wavering.

"I don't care who you are. I will not betray my people," he muttered, his voice shaking only slightly as a small stream of blood dripped from the corner of his mouth.

She reached her hand back without

looking away from him.

"The wand, Bayn," she ordered.

Bayn stepped forward and placed the rod into her open and waiting palm, his fingers grazing her flesh with heat. Taking a step back, he took a deep breath to slow his rapidly beating heart at the slight contact. Brynn heard it in her ears, the image of their brief kiss during the Victory dinner flashing into her mind for the briefest of moments. She shook her head, choosing to ignore the sudden flutter in her chest at the thought. She reached forward with the wand, letting the tip hover just over Creed's slick and bruised flesh. From what she could see, it was already beginning to heal even after only being inflicted just moments before. This also piqued her interest. The thought of what he could be intrigued her. Granted, they knew he was a Liquidator for certain, but he was also a half-breed, which could be a rather vast array of combinations. That was putting it lightly.

"I don't like doing this, Creed," she said.

Even as she said it she knew it was a lie. She reveled in the torture and the pain more than most, and some even told her it was an unhealthy obsession. What did they expect from a Daughter of Electi that had been raised by the sword? Brynn had been able to spare her younger sister from such a life and mindset, but Gwenyth had already expressed an interest in training. Brynn knew the time of her sister's innocence was coming to a close.

"So, if you just tell me what I want to

know, this will all be over," she stated.

Creed laughed, low and melodic. Beautiful.

"You mean that you'll kill me." It wasn't a question.

"I never said that," Brynn replied.

"Of course, we'd kill him," Tarren insisted, taking a step toward the two of them.

"Quiet," Brynn shouted, never looking away from Creed as she kneeled before him. Just waiting for him to give in. "When I want your opinion, Terran, I will request it. Until then, would you kindly shut the fuck up?"

Again, she held the wand over his skin, this time between his sweaty, well-defined pectorals in the direction of his heart. As he again fell under the spell of its powerful magic, he lifted his head to stare at the far wall. Brynn knew instinctively he was being transported back to some torturous recollection that he had buried in his subconscious for a long time. As the group watched in spellbound fascination, he raised his shackled hands upward, kicking out with his legs at the same time.

"Noooooooooooo," he moaned, his eyes filled with terror.

His voice had changed timbre, sounding more like the voice of a young boy. A child.

"Get off of her. Get off. Stop. Stop. Nooooooooooooo! Don't hurt her! I will kill you," he screamed.

Curious, Brynn stepped closer, shrugging off Tarren's hand on her shoulder in a half-hearted attempt to restrain her from approaching Creed. She saw Creed's body go limp for a moment, and his eyes rolled back in his head. Fearful that he might indeed slip away, she withdrew the wand. Others subjected to the same form of torture had been known to die experiencing the dark things the wand was capable of conjuring. The prisoner had revealed so much more than he had meant to already.

Brynn was naturally brilliant at analysis, and it was evident to her that the greatest fear her subject had experienced was bearing witness to the injury of those he cared about. All of his fears and dark memories seemed to center around that scenario.

She stepped back as Creed began to return to himself, thinking. Perhaps this well-formed creature she captured was worth sparing, after all. He was obviously capable of devotion on some level, which meant he was not a complete reprobate. There was something else she could not place, a piece of his essence not accounted for. Something she sensed rather than saw the evidence of. She turned and caught Natalia's eye.

Natalia, seemingly pleased, nodded as a smile crept along her lips. Leave it to Brynn to pick up on the one salient fact about the prisoner Creed that could provide the very key to his cooperation.

He had angel blood. She was sure of it. Just by the way the light shone on his skin. His fear of harm coming to others. In that context, his inconsistent behavior made more sense. Still, she had no reason to trust him. He had attacked with his forces, and even after torturing him she still had no idea why. She turned. Even though she was the shortest individual there, she could seem formidable, and her voice was thunderous as she spoke.

"Leave us," she commanded her entourage, enjoying the looks on their shocked faces. "I wish to question the prisoner alone."

"But Brynn—," Tarren and Bayn said in unison, their expressions instantly as thunderous as her command had been.

"Leave us, I say," Brynn thundered back, shutting them down.

She could tell by the way their muscular shoulders sagged that they knew how serious she was and were resigned to carrying out her orders.

As soon as she was sure that they were a sufficient distance away, she took a seat on the stone flooring, her legs crossed under her long skirt. She sat with her back against the opposite wall. As she addressed Creed, her voice took on a friendly tone.

"Now, Creed," she told him. "You and I will begin a real conversation. You may ask me a question that has nothing to do with the security of the Electi. In turn, I will ask you a question that you must answer to the best of your ability. It will be a version of the modern game Truth or Dare. Do you understand? The only caveat is that we both must choose truth for the first question."

Creed chuckled.

"And what will the dare be? The consequence?"

"Oh, I think I have that covered," Brynn smirked, holding up the wand, "but this wand will never be used on me because I will always choose to tell the truth in answer to any question you should ask me."

"I cannot believe that I am about to play a game with a Daughter of the Electi. No one would believe me if I tried to tell of it."

"Well, you are wrong about one thing already," Brynn told him, leaning forward. "This isn't really a game, though it has all appearances of one. I am glad that you have decided to play it with me. If you had refused, I would have freed your beautiful head from your neck immediately."

"I believe you, Daughter of the Electi," Creed answered, situating his massive, muscular, and nearly naked body so he was more comfortable. "So, you said you are willing to go first, and you will be choosing the truth. I am allowed to ask a question now, correct?"

"Correct," Brynn said briskly. "Now you may begin."

"Why am I still alive?" Creed asked.

Brynn almost laughed at the obviousness of the question.

"Because we are seeking information," she answered simply, seeing no reason to elaborate any further.

She wondered why he had asked that

particular question. She had expected, given the opportunity, he would have asked something of a more personal nature.

"I'm not sure that is the entire truth," Creed responded, never breaking his gaze from hers. "I think that there is something more to it. Oh, don't get me wrong. I'm not saying that you are lying, Exalted Daughter of the Electi. I know that in your mind you told the truth. But I believe there are many reasons why I am your prisoner rather than one of your *kill trophies*."

Brynn shrugged.

"Nevertheless, you've had your question, and I told the truth. Now it is my turn. Truth or consequence, Marauder?"

"Consequence," he answered without hesitation, brushing his curly thatch of dark hair away from his forehead.

Inwardly, Brynn frowned. She knew he hadn't enjoyed the torture the wand had inflicted as much as she usually would, yet he would rather endure more than give away his mission.

He was certainly a stubborn one.

"Very well, then," she said.

She allowed her gaze to travel for a few seconds up and down his well-muscled body until they rested on a scar just above his left knee. It extended up to his inner thigh. With the vampire blood that was so obviously a part of his heritage, there were few ways that Creed could be wounded that would leave a permanent mark. Placing the wand near the

101

scar would cause him to relive that particular moment of torture.

She decided to go for it.

Reaching out, she held the wand over the irregularly shaped scar, which looked almost like a shark bite. He immediately convulsed and began making the feral noises of an animal in pain.

"Aaaaahhhhhn!" he said, spittle flying in the air between them. "Uuuurggggg!"

Brynn kept up the pressure a few seconds longer, and then withdrew the wand. Creed opened his eyes, blinked twice as the sensory recreation faded, and sat up, looking at her warily.

"Well that was a nasty one," he commented, still somewhat out of breath, "You must have gotten started early learning the dark arts of torture, Daughter of the Electi. Other little girls might have had tea parties or played with dolls, but not you. I think you begged to learn how to inflict the most exquisite pain, and I believe you enjoyed it."

Brynn ignored the aspersion.

"You were trapped before, I see," she stated as she realized what his scar meant. "You damn near took off your own leg escaping. You must have been the possessor of some sort of power even still to accomplish that. Why don't you tell me about it?"

Creed leaned forward toward her. He looked angry and a leering look played over his face.

"Show me a glimpse of those beautiful

tits, and maybe I will," he said.

Brynn jumped up and whirled around, kicking Creed soundly in the side of the head.

"This game is over," she said, walking out.

CHAPTER EIGHT:
TRUTH & CONSEQUENCES

Trace Vexo wanted so badly to speak to his Guardian. While he heard around the Electi ranks that he had been busy guarding the elder Daughter of Electi as she questioned an unknown prisoner, he hoped that Terran would see him. He hadn't been able to say much after the Ignatur Ceremony but wished he had. He wanted to be confident that Terran knew he hadn't meant for him to endure such torture.

As he walked within the walls of the Electi mansion, he couldn't help but imagine the danger in progress just below his feet in the sub-basement. Regardless, he pushed himself faster toward his Guardian's bedroom. He was confident he waited there while Brynn, their fearless warrior Queen, used her masterful hand against the fiend captured inside their walls.

Before he knew it, he stood in front of

the dark wooden door to the room that housed his Guardian and mentor. He raised his small fist and rapped on the wood, jumping on the balls of his feet as he waited for the twin to reply. The door swung open, and Tarren stood on the other side looking as if he had not endured the cruelties of his childishness at all.

"Oh, Guardian," Trace stammered as he nodded his head with respect to the brother. "I have come to speak with you."

Terran smiled weakly, showing that the previous day's events had indeed tired him despite how much of an act he put up.

"Trace, yes, please do come in," Terran exclaimed as he took a step backward and motioned for the youth to enter his private chambers.

Trace made his way into the room hesitantly, stopping just inside the door.

"Oh come on, Vexo. I won't bite, and there are no hard feelings," Terran joked. "Make it quick. The Daughter of Electi could need me at any moment."

The young male nodded and walked into the room a little faster than when he had first strolled inside. The room was large, the walls covered in elegant black and white wallpaper that looked somewhat like lace. White carpet covered the floor, and the bed was so large Trace thought for a moment that four men the same size as the twin could fit on the mattress.

"I wanted to apologize for my behavior, Terran. I acted foolishly, and it cost you so much more than it did me. I can't stop thinking about your injuries," Trace stated vehemently.

Terran closed the door and dismissed Trace's apology with a wave of his large hand, looking at him with eyebrows raised in amusement. His smile grew, and he laughed softly as if Trace would not be able to hear his delight.

"There is no need for such trivial things as an apology, Trace. I am confident you have learned your lesson and won't act in such a way again. I am not worried about it and," Terran began as he crossed his arms over his broad muscled chest, "neither should you be."

Trace licked his lips nervously and shifted uncomfortably under the twin's gaze.

"I know. I cannot help it. I keep replaying the event over and over in my mind, and it's nearly torturous," he admitted.

Terran's deep and velvet laugh drifted through the room and bounced off of the walls to greet Trace's ears. The larger male nearly slapped his knee with glee at the hilarity and irony of what Trace had just said to him.

"I can assure you, son, that is the point of the Ignatur Ceremony. Mark my words, though. That won't be taking place ever again. You want to know why?"

"Of course." Trace's voice raised nearly an octave in pitch as his curiosity piqued.

The large brother sauntered over to him and placed a large warm hand on the youth's shoulder in reassurance.

"Because I need to take my charge as your Guardian even more seriously than I had before. Be prepared, Trace Vexo. You will train like no other and be better for it because you have me watching your every step. You understand me?"

The boy nodded, looking up at his mentor in wonder and awe.

"Yes, Craven Twin, I understand."

"Now," Terran said as he moved to the other side of the vast expanse of his bedroom and picked up his black leather jacket from the plush chair at the side of his bed, slipping it over his shoulders, "I must check in on the Daughter of Electi. You are welcome to stay as long as you wish. I am certain your parents cannot stand the sight of you at the moment. Take your time going home, okay?"

All the boy could do was nod at the incredibly generous gesture. Once he saw the youth's response, Terran turned and left the room, closing the door behind him and leaving Trace with his disturbing thoughts of the consequences.

Calyx watched in silence as Brynn tortured the captive, resisting the urge to join her friend in the quest for information that he was so eagerly willing to hold onto. It hadn't mattered what she did to him or what he saw when inflicted with the wand. He never divulged even a crumb of intel. Calyx had seen that coming but didn't expect Brynn's reaction to his defiance.

A game of truth or dare? No, more like a game of truth and consequences, which Calyx knew was Brynn's favorite torture method, only second to the cat of nine tails. Even severing limbs was after this nifty game. It always worked for her. That was something she couldn't deny. Calyx walked down the hallway toward her bedroom within the mansion, knowing full well that there was nothing she could do until Brynn called for them again.

"Calyx," a voice came from behind her.

Without stopping, she turned her head to find Bayn walking briskly in her direction.

"What do you want, Bayn?" she asked, not even caring to stop the disdain dripping off every syllable.

Bayn caught up to her, his long legs carrying him quickly down the hall as Calyx's door came into view.

"How could you let her do this?" he asked he grabbed her shoulder and spun her to look at him.

She turned her back against the wall and stared daggers at him as he towered over her.

"You know Brynn as well as I do. Once she has a plan, there is no stopping her. Or have you forgotten that, friend? You are so in love with her that is something you should remember," Calyx spat at him.

She felt the fury rolling off him like

smoke as his muscles curled under his perfect flesh.

Just then his muscles relaxed, and he sagged against the opposite wall.

"That woman will be the death of me, I swear it," he admitted.

Something about his demeanor caused Calyx to relent a little.

"Why not just talk to her? Tell her how you feel. You know her time is running out, and she will be forced to select a mate before long. She never talks about it, but she knows. I can see the desperation on her face at times when Natalia reminds her that selecting a Breeding Partner is one of her sacred duties. Maybe the timing is better than it's ever been," she finished.

Bayn raised tortured eyes to her.

"But she knows, Calyx. She knows that either Tarren or I would die for her. How desperately in love with her we both are. Why is she prolonging our agony? It has to have something to do with Gwenyth, doesn't it? Do you think that she wants to see Gwenyth happily paired up first? I believe Brynn fears that her sister will never find a suitable mate. Frankly, the way Brynn *mother hens* Gwenyth, she is just getting in her own way."

"It may be sooner than you think, Bayn. But answer me this. If Brynn does make a selection and it isn't you or Tarren, how will you feel then?"

"I wouldn't like it, but in spite of my personal devastation I would never leave her side, and neither would Tarren. Even if I settled down with some other female, I would probably call her Brynn's name even as we made love, but I would be willing to live with it just to be near her for the rest of my days. That is the depth of commitment I feel for her."

Calyx giggled and pulled Bayn by one arm to get him moving again.

"We will see who the Daughter of Electi selects. As for calling another female by Brynn's name, that never goes over well. You can expect to be slapped. Or worse."

Gwenyth was out of breath when she reached the wild grape arbor behind the mansion, perspiring between her young breasts and filled with the wrenching excitement that only young love can bring.

Brynn was otherwise occupied, and getting away from both her older sister and the guards that hovered over her was quite a feat. Somehow, she had managed it. Everyone assigned to her constant surveillance was sure that she was with someone else, and that gave her the perfect opportunity to arrange a clandestine meeting with someone she hoped would become her lover.

Ryder Perkins.

He stepped suddenly out of the shadows, startling her.

"I apologize, my fair Daughter of the Electi," he said bowing, a secret smile twitching at the corners of his lips and pleasure twinkling in his dark eyes. "I did not mean to frighten you. But at this time my ardor for you must be concealed, I know. I wouldn't wish you the wrath of the others, especially your sister,"

Gwenyth looked up at him. He seemed even taller, more handsome, and alluring in the moonlight than he had been by candlelight. Was that even possible?

"Are you wearing it?" he asked. "Please, tell me that you are wearing the token of my affections. You honored me by accepting it, and I am the happiest vampire in all of Los Angeles."

Gwenyth didn't answer, but reached slender fingers between her small breasts and hauled the amulet up by its chain so he could see she wore it.

"I never take it off," she told him, "and I insist on bathing alone now so the servants can't see it. Brynn finally agreed with me that I could have my privacy."

"I can't blame your sister," Ryder answered, moving more closely toward her, and inhaling the pure scent of her young skin. "You are such a beauty, Gwenyth. Such a treasure. Of course, she would be protective of you."

Gwenyth felt a thrill go through her as she instinctively raised her beautiful face, standing on her tiptoes to meet his lips as they covered hers. Their first kiss was electric, shocking her young body to life and awakening her long-dormant sexuality.

The emotions she felt created a storm inside her. She felt sick with longing. She wanted — she desired — something more.

Ryder felt her muscles tighten against him in anticipation, the longing wafting off her like churning smoke. Her body was small against his, not yet developed into the woman she would become once her full transition hit. He couldn't lie to himself and say that he wasn't attracted to her, her beauty nearly rivaling her older sister's.

The Daughters of Electi were said to be legendary beauties and, from what he had seen once he joined Brynn's brigade, it was true. Gwenyth was naive, bending so quickly to Ryder's advances that he almost felt sorry for her in a way, even with her body pressed into his with need. Her desire tickled his nostrils and caused his heart to race, but he chose to take this at a slow pace for it was a slow process — integrating himself into an already established fold. He seemed to manage just fine enough as long as he could get closer to Gwyneth to worm his way in.

He just had to make certain he wasn't becoming distracted by the younger sister. He had a job to complete. Within an instant, Gwyneth's eyes popped open, and she pulled away, her warmth leaving him just as quickly and confused.

"What is it?" he asked.

"I sensed something about that man, and now I know what it was." She took Ryder's hand in hers and began to lead him back to the basement where the Liquidator hybrid was being kept. "Come on."

While Gwenyth pulled Ryder from under the grape arbor, overcome by the charms of the male, Brynn met with Natalia. She pounded her fist on the heavy oak table in front of her in one of the School Conference chambers.

"He tells me nothing, and I have tortured him to the point of near physical death with that wand. I have never met such an arrogant, insulting, and stubborn individual in all of my days. Are you listening, Natalia? This Creed is driving me mad. It's almost like he wants to die."

Natalia looked at Brynn evenly with her mind's eye. She certainly had her father's temper and her mother's sharp tongue. It was difficult to reason with her when she was worked up.

"Perhaps you should take a different tact. Just ignore him for a while, eh? It is evident he enjoys your attention, even if it causes him excruciating pain. Just leave him alone for a while. This one is different. I think boredom might accomplish what all your torture tactics have failed to."

Brynn stared at her for a moment, stunned.

"Natalia, I am not sure if that is the most brilliant idea I have ever heard or the lamest. What if he never talks? What am I keeping him alive for? I would rather end him and not have to be bothered. He is such a thorn in my side."

"I know, Daughter of the Electi," Natalia said, making her raspy voice gentler. "But there is something you have not realized in all this. There is something he covets as he has never coveted anything in his entire existence. Though I may be blind, I can see it."

Brynn shrugged her shoulders.

"Then tell me what it is and maybe we can offer up a bribe," she said, wondering what Natalia was referring to.

She had calmed down, but she wished Natalia would stop talking in circles and come to the point.

Natalia chuckled.

"It is you, Brynn. He wants you, and he would continue to endure any amount of torture to be close to you. Surely, if you search your soul, you will realize that this is true."

Brynn's mouth formed a perfect *O*, and she fell silent. Half of her was furious, realizing that she had inadvertently given Creed the attention he sought from her. The other part of her, the part that she found herself silencing with each new encounter with the prisoner, recognized that there was something that drew her to him. A strange fascination that she would rather die than admit.

She stood abruptly.

"I will follow your advice. If this Creed character is taking pleasure in my presence, then I will make sure I stay far away from him. Thank you, Natalia."

Brynn exchanged an embrace with Natalia as she left, kissing her on both cheeks. Natalia waited until the echoes of Brynn's boot-clad retreating footsteps faded before she turned to one of the dark passages behind where she was sitting.

"You may show yourself now, Carter." Natalia tossed her hair over her shoulder as she stretched out her arms and legs before her. "I didn't mean to keep you waiting, but you know when the Daughter of the Electi asks for a meeting I must attend to her."

A young man appeared from behind the curtain. He was a recently added member of the guard, and he took his duties very seriously. He stood in front of Natalia, his long sun-streaked brown hair hanging over one eye. He then bowed in deference, taking, and kissing her hand.

"Natalia," he breathed. "I would wait longer for you. You must know that."

Natalia laughed easily. The young man in front of her was someone she had known for years. In his time he was one of the School's warriors in training that was constantly in trouble, up for disciplinary action, and almost expelled a few times as a result. Now, he was perhaps the fiercest warrior, other than Tarren and Bayn, that the School for Warrior Training had ever produced.

"Carter, what was your last kill count?" she asked.

"Forty-nine at last count, I believe," he said with a smile. "And rising with each battle."

Natalia raised her face to his so he could see the look of sheer admiration in her eyes.

"I am so proud of you, you know—," but before she could finish her sentence the youth hauled her up against him, pressing his lips to hers.

Passion bloomed in Natalia's gut, intense desire for the male flooding her entire body as the muscles just below her waist tightened in response to his mouth. She may have been blind, but her senses were keen. She sensed he desired for her as well, making his pull even stronger.

Without breaking the intensity of their kiss, the stalwart young man tucked one muscular arm behind her legs and lifted her against his chest, cradling her body as he walked out through the West passageway and toward her private chambers. He set her down in front of her massive sleeping cushions so that she could remove her layers of robes. Because she was an Oracle, no one was allowed to touch her sacred raiment but her own hands. That did not stop them.

Carter felt his pulse racing as he

watched her disrobe. It never got old. To anticipate mounting her excited him to the point of frenzy as it always had. For years after reaching puberty, he lived with a secret considered so shameful that he never allowed himself to think about it unless he was alone and could masturbate.

He was *hot for teacher,* and always had been.

As soon as the last bit of her apparel dropped onto the stone floor, he scooped her up again and tumbled with her onto her bed. Underneath her robes, she was almost petite with nipples an unusual deep rose color and masses of dark curly pubic hair between her thighs.

He buried his face between her legs, pleasuring her as she moaned. Natalia had confessed to him that she had felt his ardor from the beginning but knew that an affair was verboten. Not only by the rules of the Electi, but also by all the statues of the Gods that she served until he graduated from the Warriors Institute.

The night of the day he finally graduated, he had shown up at the door to her private chambers, unwilling to wait a second longer to see if she would have him. He would never forget how she smiled at him from under the shadow of her hood, her ruby lips curving deliciously as she reached out to grasp his manhood firmly. That was all the encouragement he needed. They had been fucking like rabbits ever since.

118

At Natalia's third moan, he moved up and lowered himself between her legs, thrusting hard into her, causing her to grab handfuls of his hair. He kissed her again, the viscous wetness from between her legs still on his lips, and kept plunging into her. She smelled like roses and stone dust and ancient tombs, and he felt that he wanted to be by her side forever.

When he finally collapsed on top of her, he knew he had found his Heaven.

Creed sat in his cell, listening to the noises of the Electi jail within the mansion's basement as he leaned back against the wall. His jaw still throbbed from Brynn's swift and irritated kick, but he could manage it just fine. He had sincerely hoped she would give in to his request, but knew she wouldn't. While he had heard many things about the Daughter of Electi, her boundaries were still unclear to him. He rubbed his jaw, leaned his head against the wall behind him, and let his hands fall into his lap, his long legs crossed.

With a sigh, he thought about how long he watched the Daughter in the shadows long before their meeting in battle at her own home. She fought valiantly each and every time without regard for her own life as long as she could slay a few Liquidators and save a few lives. That was what mattered to her. That and the Quaji. His father did know she possessed the *Sapphire Eye*, allowing her to see the soul sparks. He also knew she was collecting them, but they had no idea for what purpose. Her crimson eyes would flash a brilliant blue when the Eye was triggered, and she would remove her glass jars to collect the Quaji of the Liquidators after every battle, never missing a single one.

He didn't only admire her skill in battle, but he admired her tenacity and determination. He had seen it in her eyes as she sat in front of him and attempted to gain information she had no business with. And, Gods, she was beautiful.

He closed his eyes and pictured her sitting there with eyes intent on him, those deep red irises watching his every movement and every facial expression. He was enthralled. Had been since the first time he saw her in battle in a deep and dark alley in the heart of downtown Los Angeles years ago.

It was raining, and the Liquidators had quickly surrounded her and her band of fighters, including the Fae half-breed and the twin brothers. She had remained calm, a smirk on that lovely mouth as her fangs peeked through. Her band of fighters dispatched the Liquidators with ease, Brynn killing most of them herself with her long blade, all coiled and lethal grace. Her pale skin was perfect, not marred by a single scar or blemish, and he was certain there was a part of her that he wanted so badly to be a part of was just as perfect.

As the thought struck him, he felt that familiar clench of desire within his gut as heat spread through his body and down to his groin. He scrubbed his hand down his face, the stubble along his jaw rough on his palm.

"Fuck," he breathed.

He adjusted so his obvious arousal couldn't be seen from the outside the cell with knees tucked against his chest. He placed his hands on his knees and opened his eyes, watching the shadows from down the hallway move in the light against the wall through the iron bars that held him.

"Get your shit together, Creed," he chided himself.

There was silence for a few moments until footsteps sounded, echoing off the walls.

A head of blonde hair rounded the corner, followed by a strong warrior — one he had not yet seen. He recognized the girl instantly. Brynn's younger sister came to see him, but for what? He could smell the lust rolling off them both and knew they had been all over each other but, he had no inclination as to why they were there. A guard was close on their heels and her gaze leveled at him — her striking eyes not nearly as beautiful as her sister's. Creed couldn't help but notice their differences.

"What do I owe the pleas—" Creed began.

The younger Daughter of Electi cut him off.

"I know what you are, Liquidator, so

121

spare me the pleasantries." She turned to the guard and said, "Get my sister. I know what we need to do next. I'm certain he will have some answers."

This left Creed confused. Who was he? And what answers would he have?

Finally, for the first time since he had awoken as a prisoner of the Electi, Creed was afraid.

CHAPTER NINE:
MAKING ANGELS QUAKE

They stood in a half circle in front of Creed, their eyes solemn. Something had changed in the demeanor of the group. He could sense it. Brynn was there now. Although earlier she had interrogated him with a look of pure loathing and disdain on her face. Now, she looked more contemplative as if she were the possessor of new information.

In actuality, she was.

"Show me the Mark," she said tersely, her long hair glittering as she stood in the dim interior of his cell.

Creed immediately responded, "What mark?"

With one look into her prismatic crimson eyes, the words died on his lips. Instead, his shoulders sagged slightly in defeat. He knew no protest could dissuade his captors that they had at last discovered the one secret he had been so successful at hiding from them.

Even the smart-ass twins, Tarren and Bayn, were almost reverently quiet.

With a deep sigh, he turned so those gathered there could see something on his side, at a forty-five-degree angle from his armpit almost equidistant from his armpit to his waist. At first glance, it looked like some sort of stamp or seal. It was roughly circular, but had edges that looked to be crimped. Everyone stepped more closely toward him to get a better look.

Their eyes widened as they realized how intricate the Angel Mark was. It had the appearance of a medallion with elaborate inscriptions that fanned out from the center of it in a completely symmetrical design. Yet, it was flush with his skin. It hadn't been carved or even tattooed on him, and it was only visible when the light hit it a certain way.

"Ah," Brynn breathed.

It was the first time she had seen the Angel's Mark herself, and she had seen plenty of naked and half-naked male beings in the context of battle. She rearranged her features so as not to look impressed. Creed turned back as soon as the gawkers stepped away from him again.

"Game changer?" he suggested helpfully.

"Hah," Brynn scoffed. "Just another bit of intel, thank you. You could have saved yourself a lot of pain by being forthcoming. I don't feel a bit sorry for you. You are as stubborn as they come."

"Possibly," Creed agreed with her, pushing a lock of his hair back from his face. "Though I think I've met my equal today, Daughter of the Electi. Although I'm sure, you would call it *tenacity* instead. So can we be friends now?" he continued, a mocking tone in his voice.

"I don't make friends with beings who stink," Brynn said rudely, wrinkling her petite nose. She turned her head to shout at the dungeon wardens. "Unshackle him except for his manacles."

"Keep him in your sights, you two. Ryder, if he even tries to run, shoot him down. Gwenyth—," she growled, turning to Bayn and Tarren.

Gwenyth, whose head had been lowered lifted it eagerly, an expectant expression on her face.

"Yes, Brynn? I mean, yes, Commander?"

"Go ask that the room next to mine be prepared, and a hot bath available for our guest. Natalia," she continued, harshly, "be prepared to secure the room with a warding spell. Only those present here now will be able to access the room. And yourself, of course."

All of Brynn's surrounding staff scrambled to accomplish their tasks. Creed's facial expression alternated between astonishment and suspicion as one by one shackles and chains around his throat, waist, arms, and ankles were removed. When he stood up, the first thing he did was stretch mightily with a groan.

125

"Ahhhh," he said. "That feels good. Thank you, Brynn, Daughter of the Electi. I must say, I am surprised. I saw myself rotting here indefinitely. You know, another victim of your *hospitality*."

"Maybe you should," Brynn said coldly with a shrewd look in her eye, "but I'm curious. Perhaps with your peculiar set of skills, you might serve our cause against those whose blood you bear traces of in your veins."

The group began walking through the now open door of Creed's cell and into the vaulted hallway, their steps echoing. Walking beside Creed, with Bayn and Tarren directly behind them, Ryder Perkins led the group and walked backward every few feet without missing a step to eye the prisoner.

Creed had his hands shackled in front of him as he walked. His unruly hair tumbled over one eye until he tossed his head back. To Brynn, he seemed not as angry as he had been, but more defiant than ever as they moved him to his new quarters. Even though he was dirty and dressed in rags, he held himself as if he were visiting royalty.

Brynn stood with them in front of the specially equipped chamber next to her own. It had been a tiring day. The Twins looked at her expectantly as if waiting for further orders.

"Keep a careful eye on him," she told them. "Let the servants make him presentable. He will dine with us tonight. Do not allow Natalia's shackles to be removed from him for any reason outside of this room. You got that?"

Gwenyth floated down the hallway toward her, but before she turned Brynn took time for one last look of appraisal at Creed. He stared right back at her.

"You will do well not to disappoint me, Creed," she told him. Her voice was well-modulated, but there was a note of menace in her words. "Otherwise, I will have no trouble in separating your head from your body and tossing it to the guard to play soccer with."

Creed bowed to her. Although she took his gesture as mocking, when he straightened up, and their eyes met again he seemed serious.

"I will not disappoint you, Brynn, Daughter of the Electi. This I promise. And I will go a bit further still. I will be the one you turn to. Your champion. I believe we have much to teach each other and much to learn from each other. I want you to ask yourself this —"

Brynn sniffed disdainfully, waiting for Creed to finish. She couldn't shake the feeling that he was baiting her again, although his attitude seemed to have changed.

"—what happens when a vampire drinks angel blood? Do you know? Granted, my blood is not pure, but why do you think your people trafficked with angels as far back in history as your people go? Reflect on that and let me know what you come up with," he finished.

It was after the dinner hour, and a cool evening breeze blew back Gwenyth's hair as she exited out of a hidden side door of Brynn's mansion, running to her left where the tall hedges were.

As was her penchant, Brynn had insisted that some unusual landscaping be done on the property out back. In Los Angeles, the land was expensive, and she had insisted that not only her home but also the surrounding area be well groomed and unique as well as covert. To this end, she had instructed the master gardener to have a maze built.

Brynn had a fascination with them.

She believed as the ancients did that walking a labyrinth could provide spiritual insight and be a deeply personal and meditative experience. Her parents had taken her and Gwenyth to visit the Hampton Court Maze in Great Britain that had existed since the time of William of Orange. It left an indelible impression on both of them.

Gwenyth was not visiting the maze for the usual reasons, though. She was determined to keep meeting illicitly with Ryder Perkins away from prying eyes. She rounded the fourth blind corner, the fresh green smell of the hedges alive in her nostrils and the ghost of a pale moon starting to rise in the sky. Someone grabbed her from behind.

Ryder quickly spun her around, covering her tender young lips with his own. Ryder had been Gwenyth's secret joy for days now. She still wore the necklace he gave her. As he kissed her, his fingers moved from her neck down into her bosom to pull it up and finger it.

When he'd first given it to her, it had been as a token of his admiration. Now she regarded it as a symbol of his ownership of her heart. There were plenty of young men in the Guard who cast admiring glances at her every day. Even her Brynn encouraged her to socialize with them.

Gwenyth wasn't interested in boys. One of the most intoxicating qualities Ryder had was that he was not a boy, but a man. The thought that such a gorgeous, healthy, kind, and experienced male chose her above all others made her love him all the more desperately.

Their meetings had but one purpose in Gwenyth's mind. Ryder was teaching her the Art of Love. How to give and receive pleasure. She was more than willing to learn.

Brynn knew full well what she had to do, and whom she had to go to in order to find the meaning of Creed's cryptic request. He made it sound like she would need him in the future. For the life of her, she couldn't fathom why she would ever need a Liquidator half-breed for anything besides giving him a good beating when it served her. His words had intrigued her, and she could only think of one person who had the answer. Natalia was an excellent Oracle, smart and cunning, but this wasn't something she wanted to burden her with. Not when she could possibly handle it without her.

Leo was an angel of the highest order, the one said to thwart demons. In reality, he was an asshole with a bad temper that killed Liquidators alongside the vampires and all other creatures made by the Creator. He would have the answers she sought, but she knew she would need to bring back-up with her.

She felt Bayn and Tarren were perfect for the task. The large men were intimidating, and she had plenty of guards inside the mansion to watch over their prisoner. She was confident she'd need the muscle. Leo's club, Abaddon, was as rough and tumble as they came. Violence and darkness permeated every inch of its interior and even leaked in tendrils out to follow individual patrons home.

The name was a perfect match, representing the dark pit of despair, desperation, and drunkenness that most found themselves in when they entered the double glass doors. Brynn, Terran, and Bayn stood outside watching the flurry of activity. Abaddon was nestled in a little niche in Downtown Los Angeles, which was perfect for hiding some of the seedy activity that took place there most of the time.

"You sure this is a good idea, Brynn? What if that jerk was just fucking with you?" Terran said as he shifted uncomfortably, his well-worn leather jacket rolling with his muscles underneath.

Brynn glanced back at him, placed her hands on her hips, and turned back to squint up at the red neon sign of the club.

"Then I beat the shit out of him, Terran. It's as simple as that."

They entered, Bayn holding open the door for the other two and not saying much. When the waitress attempted to seat them, they stood instead and surveyed the room carefully. They spotted their target in a special booth built into the back of the club. The red leather seats were arranged in a half-circle and the portion against the wall had a gilded, ornately carved back that rose above the center, seating full of skulls and bats and other night creatures that looked like a throne.

Leo didn't exactly look happy to see them. Resigned, he motioned for them to join him.

"You brought your handsome goons, I see," Leo crooned.

Brynn wondered briefly which team he was playing on tonight. His eyes were thickly lined with kohl and mascara. He was also known for his mercurial and fluid sexuality.

"Hello, boys," he said as Brynn slid into the half circle on one side of the owner. "Have a seat. Drinks on me, of course. May I say that it is a pleasure to see any Daughter of the Electi in my establishment? Not up to your usual standard, I am sure. It must be something very intriguing that brings you here."

Brynn allowed the nefarious Leo to kiss her hand briefly, glad she had thin leather gloves on. Still, she felt the warmth of his tongue as he took her hand for a moment and licked the back of it.

Tarren glowered, his hand underneath the table on the handle of his dagger. He glanced over at Bayn, who looked equally tense.

Leo looked from one to the other and laughed at them.

"Relax boys," he suggested, "and order quickly. I can tell you both need a blowjob by someone who knows how. You know what? I think I will order for you, actually." He rested his hand on his chin briefly. "I have a new drink I just concocted, and I want your honest opinion."

Leo looked up and a slight female skitted forward. He didn't speak, just held up four fingers. She quickly curtsied and came back within seconds with four phosphorescent blue drinks. Leo raised his glass flute and looked at the others.

"I give you my new libation," he said, looking directly at Brynn. "Offered to the only deity that I am well acquainted with and pledged to serve."

All of them immediately took a drink.

Tarren tossed his back without tasting it and began coughing, then clearing his throat.

"Yes, it's very potent," Leo told him, smirking with delight. "I call it the *Sapphire Eye*."

Brynn tasted the drink. It tasted like rare blue raspberries with undertones of oak. It seemed to have a kick at the end of each sip. Yet, Brynn knew there was more to it than that.

"What's the secret ingredient Leo?" she asked. "I detect something else, and given the reputation of this place—"

Leo threw up his hands, chuckling.

"Okay, you've got me," he confessed. "Just the tiniest bit of Fairy Blood thrown in. For the kick, of course."

Brynn nodded.

"Great. We just cannibalized Calyx. Wonderful," Bayn said with disgust.

"Oh, dear boy, don't carry on so. Everyone knows the blood of any phylum adds loads of flavor and intrigue." Leo winked as he took another sip of the drink.

"You didn't tell us," Tarren fumed quietly. His face was still red from nearly choking.

"You didn't ask, now, did you, muscle man?" Leo replied, turning to Brynn. "I know you seek me out for a reason, my liege. I am at your service, naturally."

"I want to know what you know of angels and angel half-breeds," Brynn said, looking at him directly. "I know Natalia

133

probably knows as much as you do, but I also know that she doesn't sleep with them."

Leo took another sip of his drink, savoring it.

"Well, I do know quite a bit," he told her, "and things that you would never find written down anywhere. For example, I am sure you have no idea what expert tracker angels are. Better than bloodhounds. For that reason alone, they are often kept in enchanted chains, traveling with rogue armies."

Brynn was surprised.

"How does it work?" she asked. "I am sure you are not talking about making them follow tracks on a leash like dogs."

"Of course not," Leo said disdainfully. "Any vampire may experience and acquire the same highly evolved tracking abilities by drinking either their blood or their sperm."

Bayn choked on his drink at the revelation and covered his mouth as he cleared his throat.

"What else can you tell me?" Brynn asked unperplexed by the comment but eagerly.

Everything Leo had revealed so far was a revelation.

"Oh God, Brynn, why don't you sit back and relax? And I do ask, do not let that drink go to waste. We all know Fairy blood is hard to come by," Leo chided as he leaned back in his seat and his eyes moved over Brynn's body as she sat in front of him. "That kick isn't the only thing it does."

A sly grin moved over his lips and settled there, but Brynn wanted so badly to slap it off of his face.

"Ha, you wish, angel. A member of the Electi has never slept with an angel, and I don't see that changing," Brynn bit back. "At least," she paused long enough to tip her head back and take the rest of the libation down her throat, "not while I'm alive. Plus, you know as well as I do that the Creator deemed it blasphemous."

"Oh, but that doesn't stop anyone, now does it?" Leo replied with a snide smirk.

Leo's sly grin only broadened, and he leaned forward, his bright eyes not once leaving the apex of Brynn's crossed legs.

Bayn and Terran were becoming antsy, warmth moved over them in delicious waves as they sat and watched the exchange between Brynn and the angel. Leo was stalling, but for what reason? What did he know that he wasn't willing to share?

Bayn slammed his hand on the table between them and nearly shouted over the thumping music beating around them.

"That is enough, angel. We are not here to play games."

"Oh see, warrior, that is where you are wrong. You came to my house for information, so you will play whatever game I see fit. You hear me, vampire?"

The word vampire rolled off his tongue seductively, but Brynn didn't move. Barely even breathed as she watched a golden light shift over Leo's eyes as he stared Bayn down, the warrior in himself coming to the surface.

"I will tell you what you came here to find out, and even tell you more than you want to hear or are capable of understanding," he said slowly and deliberately. "Some of it is beyond the ken of even smart vampires but first, a dance I think. Brynn, Daughter of the Electi, will you do me the honor?"

Instinctively, Tarren and Bayn looked over to Brynn, their hands under the table on their blades. They both revolted at Leo's effrontery, but Brynn looked from one to the other calmly, and then turned to Leo.

"Of course," she said, surprising all of them.

Bayn stared at Leo through slitted eyes. He could have struck him down just for asking.

Both Terran and Bayn stood so Leo and Brynn would be able to exit the booth. The band was just launching into a slow number, full of haunting notes and atmospheric chords. It had a relaxing quality. Brynn thought to herself that if it were up to her, it would be titled something like *Sojourn to Hell*.

Once on the dance floor, Leo pulled her to himself so closely she could feel his manhood through the material of both their clothing.

"What a delight you are, Brynn. So delicious. I know this is a business dance because you understood I meant that I would only share certain facts about our angel

brethren with you, and you alone.
Nevertheless, I am enjoying our proximity. You are a treasure for the taking, oh Daughter of the Electi, with many suitors. One wonders how much longer you will wait to choose."

"That would be up to the Gods themselves," Brynn told him evenly.

She knew if they were alone and he had the power he would like nothing better than to ravage her, spill her virginal blood on the floor, and ravage her again. Then spend the rest of his immortal life bragging about it. This, among many other reasons, was why she remained a virgin. She couldn't stand the thought of any male being able to say that they had *had* the Warrior Brynn.

For all that she had sacrificed, she was proud that none could.

For some reason, a cloud passed over Leo's eyes as he continued to gaze at her. At the same time, his cocky countenance became sad.

"I had to get close to you to be able to use one of my gifts — it allows me to see into the future, and I can tell you this. The first male you will lay with will have angel blood, and it grieves me deeply to tell you this because it will not be me. The second thing I need to tell you is that this union will be born of necessity. There are wounds beyond your ability to heal, and an angel will heal you. The third thing I must tell you is the most important of all, Brynn, so listen very, very carefully. As there is a cost with everything, this union will cost you dearly. Your children will either be Gods or Monsters, and you will be hunted by a powerful witch whom is jealous of your union. This is what I envisioned as we drank the blood of the Fae Folk."

Brynn felt repulsed, inwardly coiling from Leo's embrace just as the last strains of the macabre dance song faded.

"So, that's it? Some sort of prophecy from one not known to be a prophet?"

Leo looked stunned for only a moment.

"All angels are prescient to some extent. Maybe this is a revelation to the high and mighty Electi, but even Fairy children know this."

"Why have I not heard any of this from my Oracle Natalia?" Brynn retorted, raising her voice so that Bayn and Tarren were immediately out of their seats, hands on their weapons and glaring daggers at Leo. "Surely she would tell me these things, and would have informed me of them long ago."

"Why she might keep these things secret from you, I cannot know. But here is another sad fact that you don't seem to have in your possession. Angels cannot lie. Even the Fallen ones. It's kind of a *thing*," he finished, backing away from her.

She looked perturbed, and before her well-documented mercurial mood turned to anger, he wanted to distance himself from her.

As Tarren and Bayn came up to flank her, she crossed her arms across her chest.

Brynn gave Leo one last long stare, just to make sure he was thoroughly intimidated.

"Come on boys, let's go," she said to the Twins, turning so that her hair swung in an arc as they left the noise and the smoky ambiance of the club behind them.

"Please, Gwenyth," Ryder said in a low voice against the side of her throat as he kissed it and then trailed upwards to make circles with his tongue in her shell-like ear.

"Gwenyth, I have never wanted anyone so much. Never touched anyone as beautiful as you are, my Princess."

Gwenyth could only moan as, moving down lower as she lay on the soft grass in a far corner of the maze, he lifted her skirt and began trailing his tongue up her inner thighs. He breathed slowly and the fact that she, the little sister of the Exalted Warrior Brynn Tremaine of the Electi, had managed to arouse a grown-ass man to a frenzy of passion, thrilled her beyond words.

In fact, she considered it her finest accomplishment. Let Brynn fight all the battles she craved. She, Gwenyth, had discovered her own true source of power. She was intoxicating to men. She was glorious in the fact that at that moment, Ryder would have killed anyone, promised anything, and done anything to be able to fuck her. As much as her own body told her it wanted the same thing, that particular scenario just wasn't going to happen.

For one thing, she was sure, as a Daughter of the Electi, until an appropriate match was found for her and was approved by Brynn, her virginity was considered some sort of prize. Gwenyth was sure that Natalia would pick up on it if she had sex with anyone and run right to Brynn immediately.

When Ryder's mouth found the valley between her thighs, she arched her back so he could open her nether lips with his tongue. This had become the time each day that she lived for. It was sex that she could have without sacrificing her hymen. Ryder knew precisely how to give her an orgasm. Several if she wanted them. And he was slowly teaching her how to pleasure him the same way. She had become addicted to his prurient attentions and on days when it was impossible to have a secret meeting, it annoyed her to the point of vexation.

Time passed, and when the bell in the garden chimed to remind everyone of the dinner hour, he got up and helped her to her feet. She smoothed her skirt back down over her knees.

"Gwenyth Tremaine, Daughter of the Electi, will you marry me?" he asked, still breathing heavily from their encounter.

It was difficult not to force himself on her. The Gods knew he had never been one for delayed gratification. But the fact that he was the first male ever to view the beauty between her thighs, the fact that he knew what her sacred parts looked like, smelled like, and tasted like was in his mind an astounding accomplishment. For now, it was difficult not completing the act, but he found it easy to pleasure himself when he was alone just recalling what he knew about her.

A large part of his enjoyment was enjoying the fact that Brynn was clueless about their intimacy. Sometimes when he was going down on Gwenyth, he fanaticized that he was going down on Brynn.

The truth was his ultimate fantasy was to have them both.

Right now Gwenyth was looking at him lovingly, so he took her gloved hand, the withered one, and brought it to his lips.

"Ryder you have to stop proposing to me every time we meet," she said softly but earnestly. "If you keep it up it won't seem as special when I am finally able to accept."

"I can't help it," he told her, kissing the tip of her nose. "I want you to be my wife. I am hopeful, but of course, if it upsets you I will at least try not to bring it up."

She allowed him to cup her nubile breast as he leaned in for another kiss. She didn't know how lucky she was that he was determined to be patient. He had promised the Vanguard of the Liquidators, the Tenebris Lords, Gwenyth's baby that could result from their planned union. The rewards he had been guaranteed for such a prize exceeded anything he might have felt for his own spawn.

So far, they were pleased with his progress. He'd made Gwenyth fall in love with him, and as it turned out, her knees weren't locked together like her business-minded older sisters were. Brynn had become such an asexual icon among her people that he'd even heard rumors that she preferred women and that Calyx was her partner.

Well, his instincts told him that wasn't true. He had seen glimpses of a woman's heart in their leader but also knew he had no chance of winning her favor. She was the greatest leader they could hope for, but as was usual for female leaders of nations, she had no social life and wasn't trying for one.

Well, he would take the younger sister then, and the rest be damned.

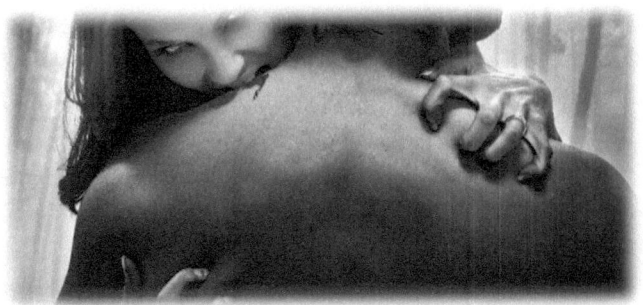

CHAPTER TEN:
FIGHTING FATE

Creed lay on the elaborately beautiful bed in his brand-new prison and, even though no iron bars or shackles kept him there, it was still a prison of sorts. Even though the walls were covered in golden paint and the sheets on the four-poster bed were white, high thread-count Egyptian cotton, he knew a prison when he was within its walls. Just because it was beautifully decorated didn't change that. Especially since there were two massive vampire guards on the other side of the door and magic layering the sheetrock. He had no illusions of freedom. Not even close.

He could not leave the room, and the dinner that was being served downstairs had been brought into the chamber and treated without care despite Brynn's insistence he dine with them. Everything had sloshed all over the plate in a mixture that looked vile but smelled amazing. The meal was made up of braised beef, green beans that were perfectly cooked, and garlic mashed potatoes, plus much more. He devoured the meal as he had not eaten since just before his capture.

All the while, his thoughts always went back to the oldest Electi daughter. Creed imagined her body as she stood in front of him in the basement holdings before he was moved. Her beauty even more legendary than he heard of before he developed his dark obsession when watching her fight against his people. His body responded quickly, his muscles tensing, and what was between his legs stiffened.

"Shit," he muttered to himself as he shook his head.

He walked into the personal bathroom located within the room, leaving the door open, and moved to the shower. Something he desperately needed.

The hum of the rising sun ran through his body, and he was confident the hot water of the shower would relieve his tension. He started the water and watched the steam come from behind the shower curtain in wave-like smoke, making the golden paint on the walls and the room so surreal he could swear he was dreaming. But no, the empty ache in his chest and the throbbing sensation below his hips told him differently. He stripped out of his clothes and left them on the floor, which was harder than he would've thought as they were coated with sweat.

Without even touching the knob that

indicated the addition of cold water, he stepped under the spray and submerged his head beneath it. He hadn't even searched for a towel to dry him once he was finished.

The urge to touch what protruded from between his legs pulled at him as the image of Brynn's high and taut breasts moved through his mind, but he resisted. He had been able to keep himself from doing so because he would not allow himself that release until he could have her, completely and utterly. Heart, soul, and body. He would not stop until he did.

What had started as a dark obsession before had turned into something he didn't want to admit to himself. He adjusted his standing position within the tub and leaned forward to place his hands on the tiled wall before him, hanging his head so the water came down in a rush down his neck and back. He closed his eyes and took a deep breath, focusing on the expansion of his lungs beneath his ribcage, and the way his heart beat when he thought of the Daughter of Electi. Hell, even just the thought of her in the same room with him made his knees weak and shaky.

Creed knew for a fact that the princess had not been mated to anyone, or even had the pleasure of a man. There was no mistaking it when he smelled the scent of lust in the air when she looked at him, the glint in her eye, and then the quick disappearance of her sweet musk replaced by irritation. There was no way possible for a woman of her stature, a pureblood vampire, to fall in love with someone like him. A Liquidator son. A breed of various creatures brought to life by the Creator. A Liquidator, a vampire, and an Angel. All of them a blasphemous mixture inside him with urges he had to fight nearly every second of every day just to follow in the footsteps of his full-blooded Liquidator father.

Footsteps he no longer wanted to follow because, if he did, it would mean the downfall of the vampires and the House of Electi. He would not see Brynn fall to that part of his nature.

Calyx waited to speak to Brynn until she returned from Abaddon. The sun was beginning to rise, and she could feel that familiar hum of it just below her flesh, causing her to rub her arms. She watched Brynn, Bayn, and Terran enter the house as she stood in the foyer with the door wide open. Calyx was tense about the Liquidator warrior being able to live upstairs within the mansion instead of a cell down in the basement where he was best contained, but it wasn't up to her. It was a decision best left for Brynn, as she was the leader of the house and the brigade she served under. That didn't stop Calyx from expressing her opinion.

Another of Brynn's soldiers came to stand beside Calyx, awaiting orders as Brynn and the Twins approached.

"Get the others and make certain that each blackout curtain is shut and that no sunlight comes in. I am shocked they haven't been lowered yet. I know you idiots can feel the sun rising," Brynn said, her voice filled with irritation at the incompetence of her staff.

Brynn ascended the front steps with the Twins behind her, flanking her as if they were still out within the city and she was in danger. For all Calyx knew, she was. She hadn't seen Brynn before she left, but Brynn was decked out in leather breeches and a halter top and looked as if she fit in within the club she just left. She would've most likely drawn the eyes of that infuriating angel Leo who ran the place.

"Brynn, I need to speak with you," Calyx began as Brynn entered the foyer and Bayn shut the doors behind them.

Brynn unhooked the top of her halter and let the straps fall, using one hand to hold the portions of fabric covering her breasts up. Brynn wasn't one for modesty despite being a virgin and nothing, or no one, stopped her from doing what she felt like, which was one thing Calyx admired about her.

"About what, Calyx? I really need you to help get the manse ready for the daylight, if you don't mind," Brynn asked, almost an order but not quite.

Calyx followed her as Brynn ascended the steps toward where her bedroom was located, the soldier she ordered to prepare for the oncoming sunlight parting ways at the bottom of the staircase. Tarren and Bayn went with him. The house became a flurry of activity almost immediately after his departure, curtains and thick velvet drapes dropping down to their rightful place covering the windows for the day.

"It's about your prisoner," Calyx admitted as they began down the hallway.

"And what about him, Calyx? I'm busy."

Calyx could tell that her leader and life-long friend was in a rush, but that didn't stop what she was about to say next. They approached Brynn's bedroom door. The door right next to it led to her prisoner with the guards in their positions on either side of the door, backs straight and hands on their pistols strapped to their hips. Brynn barely used them, but her guards were always armed with them.

"I don't think moving him up into the residence was wise. Your judgment when it comes to this man isn't sound. He needs to be placed back down in the basement where he belongs, or he needs to leave. Kill him or send him back to his Liquidator friends, but do something."

Brynn stopped in front of the door with her hand on the knob, and Calyx saw the tension move up her back and into her shoulders as her hand squeezed the metal, causing it to creak slightly. She turned toward Calyx and the crimson in her eyes was even brighter than usual against the lights in the hallway. Her lips, painted in red lipstick that contrasted beautifully with her pale complexion, were set in a thin line letting Calyx know she had deeply angered her friend.

"I'm sorry—" Calyx began, but Brynn stopped her with a wave of her hand and a look that could kill.

"I do not like my judgment being questioned, Calyx. Especially not by you. That mark on his body changes everything. After speaking to Leo, things will have to change if we are to keep gaining information from him. Do you understand me?"

Calyx was shocked by Brynn's words, and she felt the cold shock of her anger hit her square in the belly. The jolt was almost enough to knock the air out of her lungs as she stood there.

"Uh, uh, yes. I do," Calyx stammered as she swayed slightly.

Brynn squared her shoulders and pushed her bedroom door open, taking a step inside and pulling the leather halter top off of her body to drop it onto the floor.

"Now, if you could be a dear and close the door when you leave. I need to change and speak to our new housemate," Brynn said in a breathy tone.

She stepped over the top and moved toward her walk-in closet on the other side of the room. She moved much like a predator at that moment.

"Yes, Daughter of Electi."

Calyx did as she was asked. As she closed the door, her body shook with anxiety and fear. She glanced at the door beside

Brynn's, the dark wood popping out against the light blue of the walls and the plush white carpet underneath her feet.

She sighed with indignation and knew she wouldn't question Brynn's decisions. She had never steered the House of Electi in an undesirable direction during her reign. Ever. Calyx didn't see that happening anytime soon. The only problem was that Creed, the Liquidator, now shared a wall with her best friend and sister-in-arms, which could make for a dangerous situation that could very well endanger both sisters. Gwenyth was so impressionable and naïve.

She needed to find someone Brynn would listen to whose reasoning she could not deny. The image of Natalia's blind eyes fluttered into her mind, and she knew whom she needed to seek out in that instant. The Oracle would know what to do.

Calyx turned away from the doors and took off down the hallway to ready herself to make her way to the school during the daylight. It would mean using the protective clothing they sometimes used in battle, which Brynn would frown upon severely, but not more than her friend's betrayal. That thought caused her to pause at the head of the stairs and turn back slightly to look toward the guards over her shoulder. She turned back around and watched as servants and guards moved around the mansion and sighed again.

"Could you really do this?" she asked herself in a whisper. "Can you move against your friend and leader?"

The simple answer was an unfortunate *yes*.

Brynn stood in her closet and thought about what Calyx had said for a moment, the words ringing in her head as if Calyx was saying them over and over again. With her hands on her hips, she looked over her wardrobe, still fuming as she thought of her friend's accusation. That her judgment was off which, to Brynn, was an insult to her very house. The only person she had ever failed in her life was her younger sister Gwenyth, and that saddened her. Her sister pulled away from her at every turn. She was even secretive these days, so Brynn did what she could to keep the house safe, and if that meant moving the Liquidator male right next door to keep a better eye on him then so be it.

"I made the right decision. She's wrong," she said to herself with resolve.

The words still rang in her ears. She shook her head and reached for a crimson tank top, which was much more comfortable than the leather halter she had worn to see Leo. Even his own proclamation still made her head spin. That one with the blood of angels would be the one she mated. It would not be Leo himself, which saddened him. There was only one other, though not full-blooded, that was close to her. And they shared a wall.

She was attracted to him, to say the least. His broad chest and deep voice made her body burn from the inside out as she made her way to the door and opened it, turning to the guards outside the door next to hers.

"I would like to speak with the Liquidator. You can leave us, and I will get you when I am finished," Brynn ordered as she came to stand in front of them, looking up into their faces as they stared down at her.

She didn't mind being short. Had always been. What she did mind was being looked down on.

"Now," she shouted when they didn't move.

"Yes, Daughter of Electi," the older vampire stated as he pulled, the younger male away.

She watched as they walked down the hallway and took sentry at the very end with their backs toward her. With a deep and steadying breath to slow her heartbeat, she grabbed the doorknob and twisted it, slipping into the man's room without a knock or pronouncement. What greeted her when she entered was what she hadn't been expecting.

Creed walked out of the bathroom with only a plush white towel that hung low on his hips, his hair wet, and droplets of glistening water dripping down his chest. His skin was as bronze as ever, and even more delectable now that it was clean of the blood and filth that had previously covered him. Desire curled in her gut and caused her muscles to coil with brilliant tension. His eyebrows raised an inch in amusement as he took in her presence, the crimson tank top doing nothing to hide the fact she had been aroused at the sight of him.

"What pleasure do I owe this visit, Daughter of Electi?" he questioned after clearing his throat. "I was under the impression I wasn't allowed visitors."

She crossed her arms over her chest and made a conscious effort not to look at anything but the man's face which, she had to admit, nearly made her swoon all on its own. It was hard but beautiful, and elegant even with the stubble that littered his jaw.

"I spoke with Leo tonight," she replied.

Creed chuckled and ran his hand through his wet hair.

"Ah, the Angel. I know who he is. The bisexual."

The words rolled off of his tongue deliciously, and Brynn had to reel herself in.

"He told me, Creed. Well, what he knew. And what he saw. I'm not certain what to think of it anymore. I've become—"

"Confused?"

She moved to the other side of the room and inspected a photo hanging on the wall of a young woman, her mother who passed when she was only a teenage vampire. She was beautiful. Long blonde hair fell across her shoulders — the same both daughters possessed — and those same crimson eyes that Brynn inherited.

153

"Yes, if you must know."

"What's so confusing about what he divulged to you, Daughter of Electi?"

He was a lot closer to her than he had been. She felt the heat radiating off him on her back, causing a heat of her own to lick up her very center like a fire. Her body turned on instinct, her chest brushed up against him, a hiss leaving his lips as he stared down at her with the same fire that moved through her body in his eyes.

Creed took a step toward her, and she took a step back, the entire length of her spine meeting the golden wall behind her. Her breathing was erratic, and her body was entirely engulfed in the flames of the desire she felt for the male in front of her. The scent of his arousal wafted off of him like smoke that tickled her nostrils, only fanning those flames. He reached up and traced his finger along her jawline, the contact causing a shiver of anticipation to roll through her.

"See, Brynn, it is very clear that you need me to fight this war, and not just for my blood," he whispered.

He leaned down toward her, but paused as if asking permission. With one final shudder, she closed the distance between them, her lips crashing into his as her arms encircled his neck and she pressed the length of her body against him.

The taste of her intoxicated him as he pulled her closer to him. Even with them pressed together, she wasn't close enough. Creed's hand traveled up the outside of Brynn's red tank top and grazed over her breasts, her nipples hardening underneath his touch.

She moaned, and he couldn't stop himself from pushing her up against the wall. When he pulled away from her just an inch to grip her ass to lift her up, he saw those crimson eyes flash a bright and pale blue. The *Sapphire Eye*, a gift he knew she possessed so she could see the Quaji she collected. It didn't much matter to him as much as it had his father, but he wasn't concerned with that at the moment. He just needed to be closer to her.

Her hands wove through his hair as his lips pressed against her throat, a guttural growl moving up from within his throat to penetrate the air. The vampire in him began to surface as she writhed against him, but he held back as best he could. He was confident, despite the rumors, that Brynn was as pure as they came even though she loved to partake in battle. He nibbled at her throat, his own fangs throbbing as the need to puncture that gorgeous flesh of hers attempted to overwhelm him, and his arousal became even more apparent.

When her nails dug into his flesh, he growled against her lips. Her body stiffened against his and confusion overtook him, the unadulterated lust he had sensed and smelled in the air disappearing like a vacuum had been turned on in the room. Her breathing picked up as if she were in a panic and she pushed against him.

"Put me down," she said.

He pulled away from her, and there were tears in her eyes then. He opened his mouth to apologize, for what he had no idea, but she stopped him.

"Put me down, Creed."

He did as she asked and watched as she paced for a moment and then turned to leave the room, pausing before her hand met the metal doorknob. She hesitated, and he had an inclination as to why. He noticed her muscles stiffen as she stood there, thinking.

"Brynn?" he asked as confusion and concern flooded through him like a floodgate had been opened.

She turned her head slightly to look at him, closed her eyes, turned away from him, and opened the door.

"I'm sorry."

With that, she walked out and shut the door behind her, leaving Creed alone and wanting so much more than she had just given him. He wanted her to love him, and the thought that she may not be able to terrified him to his very core.

Natalia hummed as she dusted the

shelves that lined her secret closet. The door was made of six-inch thick industrial steel, and it blended in seamlessly with the stainless-steel walls of the central laboratory where Brynn stored the precious Quaji and the Zoo.

The closet — which was, in fact, her private laboratory — had been constructed by her first Warrior Graduate Student lover Actaeon. He had taken her in there once in the way that a man takes a woman, her back against the wall and her legs wrapped around his hips as he thrust into her.

She would always be fond of her secret room because of that memory.

She knew in advance that whoever contracted the secret room would have to die for her surreptitious activities to remain hidden, so she arranged for Actaeon's heart to be pierced through with an arrow during a military hunting practice. No one ever figured out how the good-looking young man found himself hit by *friendly fire* during a training exercise. Only Natalia knew because she put the arrow through the unfortunate young man's heart.

One of the great secrets of the Electi was that any issue of their royalty whether it is piss, shit, or blood was carried away, examined, and buried privately. The fact that it could contain live cells with their DNA meant that extra precautions must be taken to ensure no enemy could clone either of them.

The monthly discharge from the sacred

wombs of the Daughters of the Electi, Brynn, and Gwenyth, was the most important issue of all because it contained their unfertilized eggs. Though often released ruptured or dissolved because of the peculiar antigens of the Vampire royalty, sometimes the ovum would be passed intact.

As a trusted employee of the Daughters, they never questioned her obsession to procure this intimate material related to the future procreation of themselves. Going through it was a painstaking process that took Natalia countless hours, but it had paid off.

Lovingly, she pulled up the delicate silver chain that always rested between her ample breasts, and inserted the tiny silver key on it into a small opening in the wall. As soon as the key was placed in the lock, a drawer silently moved toward her from the stainless-steel wall, and blue-tinted vapors of liquid nitrogen rose upward. Impatiently, Natalia waved it away to look upon her prize with her mind's eye — a row of short test tubes capped with blue stoppers.

There were only five of them. Gwenyth was young yet, and few of her unfertilized ovum survived to be harvested. But Brynn, Daughter, and Leader of the Electi was another story.

For an instant, so as not to endanger them, Natalia brought them to the light. To her enhanced perceptions they each looked like supernovas, with a glowing center and ringed with a pearlescent corona of other cells.

"Power," she whispered, without realizing she'd spoken aloud.

Whether or not the Electi knew it, they were not in charge of their destiny. Natalia had taken that power from them. Regardless of Brynn or Gwenyth's decisions to wed or not wed, have children or not, she, Natalia, had the raw materials to continue their line however she saw fit. The possibilities were endless. She could even clone the Daughters of the Electi if she so desired. Impregnate herself with their offspring. Mix their DNA with that of dragons.

She sighed and gently, reverently, replaced the vials, wary that she was taking too much time. She smiled with deep satisfaction musing that regardless of how things appeared, she was in actuality the most powerful being of them all.

They just didn't know it yet.

It was just dark enough to venture out to the Poetry Garden, and Brynn, feeling disturbed at her earlier altercation with Calyx, was headed to one of her favorite places to reflect upon things and find solace.

This time of year the garden was filled with calla lilies and dinner plate hibiscus. There were climbing roses also, white, and fragrant, that had climbed the eleven-foot-tall stone walls to form a sort of bower over the ornately carved benches.

One of the benches had been a gift from Tarren on her last birthday. He had made her close her eyes as he led her through the grounds and to her favorite meditation spot. She remembered how lighthearted she had felt. It seemed like all of them had been lighthearted just a year ago. The bench that Tarren had painstakingly made with his own hands, hoping that Brynn would love it, included her name carved in ornate lettering and the inscription, *Fortissimus antique Pugnator Pulcherrima Filia Electi — Strongest Warrior and Fairest Daughter of the Electi.*

She sat down on it and threw her arm over the back, looking up at the night sky. She could hear the distant sound of traffic, but the birdsong in the gardens mostly drowned it out. She couldn't understand why she felt a rift had grown between her and Calyx lately. She knew Calyx hadn't liked being left behind when she and the twins had gone to seek information from Leo. She was also perceptive enough to know that the issues she and Calyx had centered somehow around Creed.

Was Calyx jealous? The effect Creed had seemed to have on her stymied Brynn, but surely Calyx knew she would never put anything before her loyalty to the Electi and her pledge to defend their clan.

She heard a rustling in the bushes to the side of the opening into the Poetry Garden. Was someone spying on her? Swiftly she jumped up, her jeweled dirk in her hand. What charged through the opening was not human or vampire.

The black god was huge, with mangled black hair and glowing eyes — four of them to be exact — as two heads stared back at her. It snarled and leaped upon her so quickly that she reacted automatically, quickly, driving her blade deeply into its eyes as the blood spurted all over her. Brynn managed to put out three of the eyes, but the one she missed proved her undoing, and the hellhound quickly planted its dagger-like teeth into the flesh of her small shoulder.

Ignoring the searing pain radiating from the wound, Brynn placed both hands on the blade, lowered it as far down as she was able, and slit the animal's soft underbelly open. The blade cut so deep its entrails cascaded onto her boots.

At last, it let go, wobbling sideways and then seemingly disappearing into thin air.

Brynn realized that the left side of her shirt was saturated with blood. Immediately, her head began to swim, and she stumbled forward, determined not to lose consciousness. She cursed herself for having left her cell phone in her room.

As she made her way resolutely to the back entrance of the estate, shouting at intervals for the guard. She was shocked to see Gwenyth and Ryder emerging from the high-hedged entrance of the Labyrinth. Both of them looked shocked to see her, and both ran toward her immediately. Gwenyth screamed her name.

"Hellhound," was all she could say before she fainted.

Her last frantic thought was that she was glad she hadn't looked directly into its eyes. Legend had it that whoever looked directly into the eyes of a hellhound would die.

The guard joined them even though they had begun eating the evening meal. It was at Brynn's insistence that her Guard was always served before any of the Elect members took their evening meal.

Once inside, Bayn had insisted he carry Brynn to her chambers, though she was still unconscious and bleeding copiously. Calyx, white-faced with her lips pressed together grimly, met the group at the doorway to Brynn's chambers where a hospital style gurney had been set up with small drainage ports on the side to drain off the blood.

Most of them, particularly Bayn and Tarren, had lain on the same gurney after one battle or another as they waited to heal. Never Brynn. Brynn always seemed to defy the odds. Even when she was injured severely, her vampire body appeared to rally and heal her quickly.

Something was wrong this time. *Very* wrong.

Natalia burst through the group, nearly knocking Ryder and Tarren off their feet in her rush to get close to Brynn. Her eyes were hooded, but her voice trembled as she caressed the side of Brynn's face.

"She is dying," she whispered. "This creature was enchanted, and its bite is lethal even to vampires. How the Liquidators gained such an ally, I cannot imagine."

Calyx, usually calm and in control, lost it.

"Shut up, old woman," she railed at Natalia. "Do something. She is still breathing. Earn your keep."

Natalia turned toward Calyx.

"This is not of my doing, you impertinent pixie," she spat. "Keep a civil tongue in your head or I will make sure you have no tongue at all."

As Calyx continued to fume, her chest heaving, she said, this time sounding like a wailing child, tears rolling down her cheeks, "Please do something. Heal her, please. I can feel her slipping away."

Natalia seemed to hesitate then as she started to speak again as part of the Guard burst into the room.

"The Third Quadrant on the north side of the manse had been breached. We have the Liquidators at bay for now, but we need the Elite Guard, the Royal Archers, and our Warrior Queen."

Tarren, who was Brynn's First Lieutenant, turned. He was officially in charge due to Brynn's incapacitation.

"Take the Orange Squadron and hit them back hard," he roared. "Use the

Lightning Nets if you must and fry their asses. Tell the others we are coming."

The others had been so distracted that it was a shock when the Guard turned, unblocking their view, and they suddenly saw both Natalia and Creed standing in the doorway. No one had even realized Natalia had left the room until that very moment. Both Bayn and Tarren drew their swords. Calyx whipped out her bagh naka and got in a defensive position.

"What the fuck, Natalia?" Bayn shouted, saying aloud what the others were thinking. "What the Hell is he doing here? Have you lost your fucking mind?"

Natalia was very matter-of-fact as she quickly pulled Creed forward toward the gurney by his wrist chains. Creed looked determined as he strode toward Brynn's still body. Peering over into Brynn's face, she quickly motioned to Calyx and Tarren to lift Brynn's head and shoulders slightly. Brynn's shoulder was still gushing, sending rivulets of blood over the stainless-steel surface of the gurney and into the trenches.

Natalia clicked her thumb and forefinger together. A plume of violet smoke appeared under Brynn's nostrils. As she breathed it in, she coughed and choked as her eyes fluttered open. Natalia wasted no time once she saw Brynn was awake, if not exactly alert.

"Brynn, Daughter of Electi," she said in a commanding voice. "You are dying from a hellhound bite. Unless you accept the blood of this being standing before you, and quickly, you will die. Do you understand?"

Brynn's crimson eyes seemed to move to her left, and focus on Creed's face.

"Oh," she said in a small voice. "You."

Despite the severity of the circumstances, Brynn's voice caused him to smile.

"Brynn. Brynn, you must drink from me," he crooned, his deeply masculine voice rumbling in her ears. "Natalia says it is the only way you can live to fight. Your family needs you. Your people need you."

At that moment, Natalia had had enough of talking. She rudely grabbed Creed by the back of his neck and shoved him down so Brynn could access his jugular vein. As Brynn reacted almost instinctively, driving her fangs into Creed's neck, he trembled and finished his comment with a sentence that only the two of them could hear,

"I need you," he sighed against her.

The sensations that he experienced as Brynn fed on him, weakly at first and then with surprising vigor, were inexplicably erotic. At once, he felt full of purpose, aware that a part of himself, his mongrel blood, flowed into the most beautiful woman he had ever seen. That she was drinking him into herself, forming a mysterious connection that frightened and excited him at the same time.

At last, she pulled back. Seeming to focus as she looked at the faces gathered around her, her eyes finally coming to rest on

Creed's face.

"What the Hell?" she said, pulling her small knee up to shove her booted foot against Creed's chest, catching him off balance and pushing him backward, "Have you all gone mad? I feel fine."

Bayn, Tarren, and Calyx exchanged relieved smiles. Not only was the Warrior Daughter of the Electi back, but she was back in rare form. Tarren briefed Brynn as she ran to gather more weapons from the racks in her chambers, passing some of her finest out to the others. Natalia grabbed Creed's chains and led him out of the room. He attempted to catch Brynn's eye, but she never noticed. She was completely preoccupied with the crisis at hand.

"Wait. I want to fight," Gwenyth called after Brynn as she left with the others.

Brynn whipped around and fixed her sister with a glare that froze Gwenyth in her tracks.

"No. You are not ready," she barked, adding, "and don't think I didn't notice where you came from and who was with you after I was bitten, sister. You have a lot of explaining to do."

"Make sure she goes nowhere," she added, nodding to the chamber guard.

Brynn looked grimly at the horizon toward the north. The smell of frying

Liquidator flesh — a scent of sulfur mixed with dog shit — assaulted her nostrils.

Her first thought was twofold. If they had to use the lightning nets to drive them back, there had to be hundreds of them. So this was a massive effort by the Liquidators. Her second thought was that they must have invoked dark magic in the form of a shield or a curtain because the scope of the battle was definitely outside the grounds of the Estate, and not a single human seemed to be aware.

"It's urban warfare this time," she told the others. "Bring everything you have at your disposal. Including the Zoo. Now, fly."

As the others flew off, knowing Brynn with her speed would overtake them before they reached the front lines. Brynn turned to Calyx who had known instinctively to remain behind.

"Brynn, I still have your back," was the first thing out of Calyx's mouth as they faced each other. "You must believe that."

"I do not question your loyalty, Calyx," Brynn told her soberly.

She saw trails of tears silently cascading down Calyx's beautiful face, and there was anguish in the fairy's eyes.

"I know," Calyx told her, feeling guilty suddenly for some of the thoughts she'd had of late, "but I fear for you, Brynn. There is something between you and our prisoner Creed. A kind of dark cord. I am of the Fae Folk. I know that means your destinies are somehow entwined. In our tongue, it is called a Fulcra. I know that means that you will never be rid of him, and that frightens me."

Brynn sighed, and as the two women embraced, she whispered in Calyx's ear.

"The Fates are fickle, but I love you better than a sister. I need you by my side. I would have died countless times if not for you. Do you think I do not carry these memories with me always? If you are right about the Chimera, then so be it. It has nothing to do with our connection with each other. If it is true, I will need you to be by my side more than ever, won't I?"

As she felt Calyx nod, Brynn knew it was time to overtake the Phalanx that had gone out before them. They took to the air resolutely, determined to defend what was theirs.

Gwenyth sat at the end of her beautifully appointed bed, kicking at the carpeted flooring with one bare pedicured toe. Even though the sleeve she had on her withered arm was the white silk one and her dress was short-sleeved, she still felt hot.

In the distance, she heard the noise of the far-away battle. Judging from the direction that the war cries, booming sounds, and the ear-splitting crackling noise of the lightning nets were coming from, Brynn, Tarren, Bayn, Calyx, and the others had pushed the Liquidator forces back into the city. Certainly

Fountain Avenue and undoubtedly to Echo Park.

When she heard thumping and familiar shrill cries on the roof, she quickly jumped up to run out onto her balcony. Backing up so she could see the roofline better, her heart began thumping wildly. It was the *Zoo*, the part of the Electi forces that Natalia had been in charge of developing. She had cloned many of the creatures long thought to be extinct.

Each was implanted with a tiny transmitter to control them en mass to strike on command. From what she could make out, as several of them took short turns around the manse to stretch out their leathery wings, there was mostly the genus known as Pterosaurs, including many Pterodactyls. Some had massive jaws and long fang-like teeth. Others had pronounced claws and curved sharp beaks. All of them could fly. That must be the point, Gwenyth reasoned. She involuntarily shivered at the thought because that meant this attack was larger and more vicious than any they had seen in the space of a year.

She started as the terrace of the balcony shook directly behind her. Instead of a Pterodactyl, she found herself facing Ryder. He immediately gathered her in his arms, kissing her mouth with the fervor accorded to those preparing to charge into battle.

"How?" she asked him when he finally let her up for air. "How are you still here?"

"I was left behind to ready the Zoo," he

told her smiling. "So, I thought I might check on my girl. That was certainly a rude interruption we had earlier, I have to say."

Gwenyth smiled back at him, but it was a worried smile.

"Ryder, I think Brynn knows. I was hoping in all the confusion she wouldn't wonder what we were doing in the garden, but she has never been slow on the uptake. I am convinced that after they have run the Liquidators off again, she is going to have a lot to say to me. I am not looking forward to it," she finished breathily.

Ryder kissed her again.

"Not even the Warrior Queen Brynn, Daughter of the Electi, can keep us apart, Gwenyth. You are a grown woman now. You are capable of making your own decisions. What's she going to do? Make you wear a chastity belt? Keep that beautiful quim of yours under lock and key?"

Gwenyth giggled.

"You are right, my love. You know how intimidating she can be. She has a temper too. She always ends up shutting me down, and I hate it."

"Look, my precious," Ryder told her, kissing her again as he fondled her breast. "We need no one's permission. Now or ever. So talk to your sister and see what she has to say. If she is reasonable, we will play by her rules. If she is not, we will play by ours."

Gwenyth knew he had to go, so she hurriedly kissed him.

"Show me," he said sternly.

Gwenyth lifted the chain from between her bosom and showed him the gift he'd given her.

"And show me the other," he said, smiling a sexy smile that made her melt. "Show me the gift you will give me, Gwenyth."

Shyly, Gwenyth raised her dress in the front, just high enough so he could glimpse the deep valley of her femininity.

"Ah," he said in a throaty voice. "Mine."

With a wink, he was gone. Gwenyth heard him shouting orders overhead again. Her heart fluttered in her chest watching him leave amid the rustle of giant leathery wings and shrill cries of giant flying reptiles bent on destruction.

What if he were hurt? What if he didn't return to her?

Not even the Gods could be so cruel, she decided.

Bayn ordered the others to use the lightning nets to their advantage, taking out large droves of Liquidator soldiers in the process. Now the air smelled like shit and rotting meat, and all of them were covered in their black blood, their skin slick and warm. He still had not figured out how they had breached the walls, but they had, and they had one Hell of a battle on their hands. With the Zoo coming, it would mean more magic to cloud the human minds that would most likely hear or see the action.

Bayn was not only driven by adrenaline, but by the fact that Brynn had nearly died and was brought back to them by the blood of the Liquidator mutt. It sickened him, but he took his job within the Electi ranks seriously and would not let it deter his loyalty.

Three soldiers dressed in leather slacks and long coats approached him. He removed his sword from its sheath, willing to take them head-on on his own while the others were preoccupied with their horde. They had brought another Hellhound that seemingly contained the same type of magic or poison that nearly killed their leader. He was certain Brynn would want to take the Hellhound on herself. Maybe even take one of the Liquidators prisoner for information about their purpose there tonight.

Bayn approached the men who came toward him, swirling his sword in the air in an attempt to intimidate them. It didn't seem to have the desired effect. They ran toward him, and he slashed out with the blade, slicing one just across the belly — his intestine spilling to the ground in a display of black and pale pink gore.

He lashed out at the remaining two that came for him, but missed them even with his accuracy. He was slightly distracted by the blood-covered Daughter of Electi fighting close by. She fought valiantly and as gracefully as always — her beauty never once marred by the look of murder in her eyes.

He struck out with his sword again and impaled one Liquidator in the heart with the blade, moving on to the next. He quickly dispatched the soldier with a blow to the neck that nearly decapitated him. He chanced a glance at Brynn and their eyes met, his twin brother fighting in the background behind her as the high-pitched screech ripped through the air signaling the *Zoo* had arrived.

Brynn looked up into the air and smiled as she spotted one of the creatures Natalia had brought back from extinction and magically altered to help build their army, knowing they would need reinforcements when a large number of Liquidators came calling. Blood had begun to dry on her skin and clothes uncomfortably, but the sweat from her battle caused it to become slightly liquid again. Her hair dripped down into it, enhancing the red streaks already running through her blonde locks.

Her crimson eyes glowed in the darkness as Brynn took in the appearance of the creature. Ryder ran outside to greet them, coming from inside the mansion as more of the Electi soldiers continued to push the enemy back.

"The cavalry is here," Ryder proclaimed as he pulled his blade from its scabbard and ran down toward them.

One of the monstrous beings swooped down and picked up one of the Liquidators that came running at them again. The man screamed into the night as the monster's giant claws clutched him. The creature bent down with its massive head and snapped off the Liquidator's head, squeezing it between its dagger-like teeth like a watermelon. Brynn heard the cracking sound as black blood spilled onto the ground.

A maniacal laugh left her lips as she watched the bloodshed and planned to inflict more of her own. She felt wonderfully rejuvenated by Creed's blood. She knew it was because of the Angel blood within him, and she felt like she could take on the world with her bare hands. She ran toward the wall that had been breached. A couple of Liquidator soldiers emerged from the near dark beyond it, and a sly grin spread across her lips.

"Oh, yes," she muttered to herself as they approached her.

One ran back through the massive hole when he spotted the creature, and the other pushed forward, coming at Brynn with his sword raised.

She approached him and kicked out, striking him square in the belly. He didn't double over, and he didn't stop. He raised his sword again and brought it down, and Brynn moved hers up to meet his. A clang of metal sent sparks flying at the sheer force of the strike. A shock moved through the metal, and both dropped their blades to the ground with a startled cry. While the Liquidator made a grab for his sword, Brynn continued to strike him with her bare fists. She lashed out. Her fist connected with his temple, sending him to the ground in a heap. He jumped up, and she came at him as he backed away from her, his back meeting the stone wall.

Her hand gripped his throat, and she squeezed with all the strength within her muscles. Once she heard and felt the crack of not only his spine but his larynx, she laughed even though blood flew from his open mouth to land on her face. It didn't bother her. Without a second thought, she dropped his thick body onto the pristine lawn and stalked through the rubble of the wall and out into the street where she had seen another Liquidator run. She spotted him not even twenty feet away as the light from the street lamp illuminated her. He weaved in and out of traffic, but he was no match for her.

Brynn reached backward and removed a throwing knife she had shoved into the waistband of her pants, throwing it into the air with a flourish and catching it all for show. She focused on the back of the Liquidator, but before she could throw it, she felt a jolt move through her entire body and stumbled back a few paces. Her knees shook and nearly gave out on her as she stood in the middle of oncoming traffic. Horns honked in shrill shrieks around her, and the Liquidator was getting away.

"Fuck, what the Hell?" she cried out as

another wave of something powerful and magical moved through her and came to settle in a place she didn't believe was even possible during battle.

Her muscles clenched, and her belly tightened as arousal took over. As soon as her feet hit the concrete of the sidewalk that would take her back to the mansion of the Electi, Bayn came out of the foliage. His eyes met hers and it was like the same electric zap of energy moved through him as he stared at her, his lips parting and his breath coming quickly as she watched his muscles clench before her. After all that time, she had never once seen Bayn in a sexual light except that one night in the garden. Something inside her moved her to near agony as a mysterious energy ran through her entire body.

As it would seem, it did through him as well.

CHAPTER ELEVEN:
WANTON

Moving in synchronicity to an unspoken plan as though they were in a dream state, both Brynn and Bayn entered the manse through a side door, pushing past the sentries as though they were invisible. Their boots echoed in the wide hallways. There was no conversation because there was no need for any.

Their trajectory was mutual.

Brynn kicked open the door to her chambers with one boot soaked with black Liquidator blood. She kept walking toward her pristine bed, toward the piles of damask and silk. A cut on the side of her cheekbone slowly healed itself, though a trickle of crimson flowed down her neck to her bosom. She shucked off her boots, and tore off her battle-worn clothes, dropping them on the floor as Bayn stood closely behind her.

When she was completely naked, she moved around, fixing him with the luminous look in her crimson eyes.

"Now you," she said as he stared at her beauty.

Her beautiful tip-tilted breasts were still heaving with the exertions of the battle. She was soaked in sweat from her exertions, oozing a fragrance that was beyond intoxicating — some blend of musk and tiger lily. Bayn felt raging lust course through his veins as he ripped off his battle tunic, his suede boots, and his breeches.

There was nothing to say, so he said nothing as he picked her petite, though lush, body up in his arms. Bayn placed her on the huge bed, pausing only greedily to take one of her orangey pink nipples in his mouth, then the other, in a way he had only allowed himself to imagine over the years as he yearned for her and yearned to be close to her.

They were kissing then, and their prolonged kiss took him back to the night in the garden when they had kissed for the first time. He recalled that moment many times since on nights where sleep eluded him, reaching down to pleasure himself as he imagined taking the fantasy further in his mind. Now he was beside her, both of them shamelessly naked. To his surprise, Brynn reached down and ran her fingers over the length of his manhood, pausing to caress the cobra-like head of his appendage. She smiled and searched his eyes.

"I knew you were big," she said smugly.

Bayn found himself completely

entranced, aroused beyond comprehension.

He bent his head, trailing his tongue down from between her breasts, circling her navel, and down lower to the apex of her thighs. Brynn shivered in anticipation as he hovered above her in between her legs. As he looked up at her, her gaze never wavered. Those beautiful crimson eyes never once looked away from him. This only heightened his arousal and his awareness of what was happening between the two of them. Something that he had wanted for a long time. Something his twin brother wanted for himself, but now lost his chance. If they followed through and he took her purity, she would be bound to him forever. As long as they lived.

Excitement at the prospect roared through him as his desire to take her grew exponentially. Just the thought of it caused his body to shake as he hovered there, just above one portion of her perfection. He was beyond ready to have a taste, and he was willing to bet with anyone that she tasted as beautiful as she smelled. He could no longer take the anticipation and placed the very tip of his tongue where he knew she wanted it to go, swirling gently around her arousal. An animal growl escaped him, and he closed his eyes as the taste of her spread from that point and into his mouth, coating his tongue.

He felt her hands comb through his hair and then tangle in it in her ecstasy, her breathing coming quick and short as he heard her heartbeat in his ears. It was fast and beating erratically, matching his own within his chest. He opened his eyes and gazed up at her. What he saw had him in awe. Brynn's head was thrown back, her back arched elegantly, her breasts pushed out, and her hips writhed beneath his mouth.

One word rang out in his mind as he looked up at her. *Mine.*

Bayn removed himself from his position before her and covered her body with his, causing her to arch her back against him. He shuddered and covered her mouth with his, his appendage throbbing with the need to accept the gift she offered him. All thoughts of the battle happening below them had left him as soon as he felt that flash of heat move through his body. The need to make her his mind, body, and soul took over any other impulse he may have had. Now, at that moment, all he wanted to do was mate her and take her as his own. The thought never wavered once.

He pulled away and looked into her eyes, her crimson orbs pulling at him and taking him under the wave of her spell never to surface again. And he was perfectly content with that. The smell of her soaked into his flesh, musk and lilies blanketing him. Claiming him. All of him.

Her hand came up to push a few loose strands of his dark hair from his face, nothing but love in her eyes.

"Bayn?"

The sound of his name on her full lips drove him wild, and he nearly came right then but reeled himself in. There was only one true way to claim your mate. If that happened, he wouldn't be able to make certain other males knew she belonged to him. That he belonged to her completely.

"Yes, Daughter of Electi?" he asked, a wicked grin spreading over his lips.

Without warning, she hooked her leg behind his and rolled him over onto his back as if she had done it a million times, but he knew different. Instinct drove her actions, not experience. She sat up and straddled his hips, his erection pressing against her slick flesh just between her legs. She moved against him and sweet, electric pleasure ran rampant through his body, spreading from where their bodies touched. They moaned together.

Brynn removed herself from him, and he reached out for her. Once her feet touched the floor, she leaned over his waist and ran her slick, pink tongue up his shaft. Without a second's hesitation, she took him into her mouth. He couldn't tear his eyes away as heat licked at every inch of his body and sweat broke out over his flesh. She moved up and down on him, sucking and teasing with her tongue at just the right intervals, causing him to get so close to the edge and fall back down as she retreated. As he watched her, she was a vision of sexuality, her pink nipples erect and a blush of pink across her chest from her arousal.

181

He couldn't take any more torture, and he had to claim her, and he had to now. He sat up, and she pulled away as if knowing what he was doing. His large hands grabbed her hips, and he lifted her from the floor, rolling as he tossed her back onto the bed amongst the luxurious sheets. He was on top of her within seconds. Brynn's cheeks were flushed, and she glittered with perspiration, her breaths becoming ragged and deep as she stared up at him in wonder.

"I love you, Brynn," he admitted to her, the three words never once left his lips before the moment. "Always have. You are mine."

She smiled up at him warmly, her nails raking his back lightly.

"Then take me, Bayn. Claim me," she whispered.

His body hovered over hers and the tip of his erection pressed against her entrance. He leaned down and kissed her again, pushing into her just barely. He felt her unbroken hymen just inside.

A loud and electric cracking sound penetrated the air. A red light flashed between them, sending Bayn backward and into the wall opposite the bed. A magical connection had broken like the break of a snapped rubber band. He fell to his knees and blacked out just as Brynn rose from the bed, covering herself as she moved toward him, terror plain on her face. He brought himself to a sitting position, shaking the confusion away as the urge to claim Brynn left him just as suddenly as it came. From the look on Brynn's face as she wrapped a sheet hurriedly around herself, she was just as confused as he was.

Images flashed through his mind. At first, he couldn't make them out, but then he recognized the blonde head of Gwenyth. Then the unmistakable scent of iron as blood poured across pale flesh. A feminine cry was the last thing he heard before Brynn's excited shouts brought him back to focus.

"Bayn, are you okay?" she asked as their eyes met. Bayn couldn't help but think that Brynn was beautiful even when she was afraid, the fear turning it into a tragic beauty. "What the Hell was that?"

Bayn shook his head and did not have an answer for her.

He took a profound, and steadying breath as the pain from the impact began to leak away.

"I have no clue, but your sister is in trouble. And so are the Quaji."

Brynn moved away from him quickly and shoved her body into the clothes she had shamelessly thrown to the floor in a trance that she still did not understand. Sprinting to her dresser, she grabbed all the glass vials she could, looking at Bayn with a beseeching look in her eyes. He jumped from the floor and followed in her footsteps. They exploded from the room, running as quickly as they could out of the large double doors of the mansion, their feet meeting the grass of the front lawn.

She nearly fell as her feet met the grass,

slick with Liquidator and vampire blood. What she saw around her was the most debilitating sight she would ever see in her long life. Bayn watched with confusion as her crimson stare flashed Sapphire blue, activating her gift as she looked on at what he couldn't see.

"Bayn, I have failed us," she breathed, barely audible.

Each soul spark from every slain body littering the lawn of the Electi estate floated into the air, fading one at a time as they moved into the afterlife — taking the vampire's chances at replenishment with them. There would always be more, but each was a precious gift given by the Creator, and she had left them to fade without fulfilling their purpose.

Something had caused this, and she had to find out what.

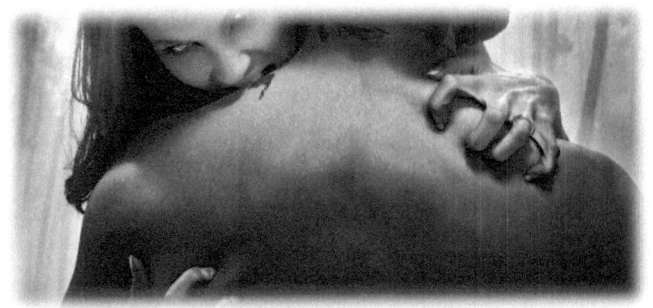

CHAPTER TWELVE:
PRECIOUS GIFTS

Ryder was wounded, but not badly enough to require medical attention. He had removed the arrow from one of his well-developed pectorals himself, and one glance at it told him all he needed to know.

Brynn was on to him, and he was a marked man.

The arrow he had removed from his immortal body was topped at the non-business end with red and silver feathers — it had been friendly fire that had nearly taken him out. If it had been embedded a little more deeply, it would have pierced his heart. He was almost sure that Calyx fired it off at Brynn's order.

That meant that he had limited time to implement the rest of his plan before he left, and he might as well do it now while the distraction of the battle was still ongoing. He looked around to see if any of the other guards or notables were observing him. He didn't see Calyx and her arrows, but he did see Tarren off in the distance, the huge hulk of a warrior vanquishing Liquidators three at a time with ease.

He half-ran back to the manse. As he approached, he was delighted to see Gwenyth outside her guarded room on her terrace, staring moodily down from her balcony, still dressed in the same virginal white gown as she had been wearing earlier. He could have flown, but he knew his boots might make a noise when he landed. So, using his massive strength, he climbed the rugged walls up to her balcony, throwing one leg over the railing, then the other, and easing himself soundlessly onto the terrace.

Gwenyth's back was to him. He crept up soundlessly behind her, first glancing to make sure the guards were outside her chambers and not in it.

"Love," he murmured as she first started, then sank back with relief into his arms, "I have returned to you."

Gwenyth spun around, and held him tightly.

"Thank the Gods," she muttered, a lone tear trailing down her cheek in relief. "I thought they might have killed you. I know my sister suspects us now. I am afraid of what she might do to keep us apart, Ryder."

"I believe she tried to kill me, Gwenyth," he told her, pulling his tunic aside to show her his wound, "Look. This is the arrow I pulled out."

Gwenyth's expression became shocked as he pulled the offending arrow out of his scabbard. It was still streaked with his blood on the end, though his wound had healed.

"How could she?" Gwenyth hissed, her voice trembling in anger. "How *dare* she? She acts so prim and proper and cold, but I see how she tortures Tarren and Bayn with her body. Always making sure they catch a glimpse of her thigh or her breasts — she knows it drives them mad, but she gets off on it! Now I fall in love, I who have never been with a man, and the bitch tries to murder you on just the suspicion that we are having an affair? It is intolerable."

"Shhhhhh now, my beauty," Ryder said, looking around.

He saw the dregs of the ongoing battle with the last lightning net arcing gracefully through the traffic on a corner of a city street and burning the Liquidators. He knew the Guard was stationed outside Brynn's chambers, but he had a plan.

"Up you go," he said to her, smiling and swinging her around so she was on his back with her legs around his waist. "I am taking you down the wall. Do not be afraid. I am a strong climber and I have done it wearing backpacks that weigh more than you do. Where can we go to be alone, Gwenyth? We need to think, and I need your warmth, my love."

"The stables," Gwenyth said, her sweet

breath on his neck giving him a pleasant tingle. "No one is there at this hour and all the hands were recruited to the battle today. We can be alone there."

Slowly and carefully, Ryder made his way down the wall. He didn't want to attract the attention of the Guard stationed on the roof by flying, but clambering down the stone-studded wall of the manse and staying in the shadows he knew he wouldn't be seen. His heart raced. At last, he would be alone with Gwenyth, Daughter of the Electi.

When he reached the ground, he put his hand to his lip so that she wouldn't speak, and slowly, still keeping to the shadows on the blindingly sunny day, he managed to keep them secret until they ran the last few feet to the entrance to the stables.

Inside it was cool and smelled of newly mown hay and eucalyptus, which the stable hands used when they mucked the stalls to rid the place of the odor of horse dung. It was pleasant, and soon Gwenyth, who knew the design of the stables from her riding lessons, took Ryder's hand and led him to the very back stall which hadn't been used in months. In one corner were half-opened bales of hay, much of it spread on the grayed and weathered boards of the flooring. A shaft of light poured down from a casement window, and they turned to each other eagerly.

Ryder broke apart from kissing her to make a request.

"Gwenyth, my bride-to-be, I want to see

you naked."

Partly out of spite for what her sister Brynn had done, and partly out of her own desire to be as close to the man she loved as possible, Gwenyth quickly removed both her gown and her underskirt. Her pert young breasts with their large rose-colored nipples bobbed as she did so.

When she was completely nude, she turned slowly in a circle, enjoying the feeling of his eyes visually drinking in every inch of her. He sat down on the piles of hay, pulling her across his lap, nuzzling her neck, and then exchanging deep kisses with her. His hand that was not holding her against him teased her breasts and then drifted down between her thighs. As soon as it did, Gwenyth gave a deep sigh, opening her thighs so he might explore her nether regions with his hands.

She was wet, drenched in anticipation of receiving him inside of her. For a moment, he was tempted nearly past his capacity to resist fucking her lush little body. Then he remembered his future depended on what he did next, and he whispered to her.

"Gwenyth," he began, his fingers still making lazy circles around her labia that became increasingly swollen and protruded in preparation for coitus.

"Yes?" she answered in a breathy voice. "Ryder, take off your clothes, my love," she added, almost petulantly.

At that point, she wanted nothing more

than a grudge fuck against her conniving and cruel sister.

"Gwenyth," he said again, looking down into her guiltless eyes, "I cannot take you as a man takes a woman now. You know to the Electi this is a marriage vow, and I will not take you to wife in a stable, my Princess. But I do ask for your maidenhead for my own. I will take it in such a way that you are still mine forever, though we have not lain as husband and wife. Will you allow me to do this? I promise I will be gentle, and I will keep it with me always. I'll keep it wrapped in my clean kerchief next to my heart. We belong to each other, Gwenyth. I need this permanent token of our love for each other. May I?"

Gwenyth looked back into his eyes, and he could see that hers were misting over.

"Yes, Ryder Perkins, my lover. You may have my virginity in any fashion you care to take it. My heart, my soul, and especially my body, are yours. I shall desire no other until the day I die."

Ryder felt himself relax then. From every standpoint, morally, spiritually, and most importantly by the rules of the Electi, Gwenyth, Daughter of the Electi was giving him permission to pop her cherry. It was a prize more valuable than diamonds to what would be his new masters, and the little lovesick fool was throwing it away with both hands.

Ah well, he mused, *that was youth for you.*

He bent his head again, covering her mouth, his tongue dancing furiously as he slowly worked on opening. For the first time, the virgin stretched across his lap, shoving her breasts up at him to suck. Like most of the Daughters of the Electi, her hymen was intact and tough. He worked his fingers so he might break it while keeping most of it intact. It was tougher than even he thought to finally get a finger inside her, and he remembered belatedly the legends that Daughters of the Electi were Hell to break for the first time but were insanely fertile.

Ryder kept up a steady stream of whispers, telling her what a gift she was giving him. He told her how brave she was, and that he didn't want to hurt her — assuring her that it would be okay. In the end, he just got tired and plunged into her with two fingers, making her cry out.

Immediately, he captured the crescent-shaped viscous prize in his handkerchief, putting it away carefully as Gwenyth moaned and tears leaked from the sides of her beautiful eyes. He looked down and saw she was bleeding copiously, her virginal blood warming his knee and turning the golden straw beneath both of them crimson.

"There, there," he told her, holding her against his chest. "That's my brave darling. And now you are mine, Gwenyth. We belong to each other forever."

"I love you," Gwenyth told him, kissing him, "I am glad, but it hurt more than I thought it would."

Just then they heard soldiers returning. They were still at a distance, but coming closer with each second.

"Up you go," he crooned.

She seemed a little unsteady on her feet, so he hurriedly helped dress her, replacing the few items of clothing she had been wearing. Ryder realized he had a dilemma. He couldn't fly her back to her room because the returning troops would see him. He couldn't climb again for the same reason, and she was bleeding enough she would bleed over his shirt and breeches if he put her on his back again.

Gwenyth sat on a bench, studying his face. When his eyes found hers, she gave him a wan smile. With her hair tousled and her face flushed, she suddenly looked like the very young, impetuous girl she was. She had no idea what she had just given up, and how dearly it would cost her.

He fell to his knees.

"Gwenyth, the soldiers are returning and if they find me here, they will kill me. Can you figure out some way to get back into the residence? I'm sorry, but I cannot return you."

She reached forward to stroke his hair.

"Of course, I can. I shan't have you killed trying to help me get back to my room. I might be able to go through the kitchen. But you must leave. Now, my love. Just promise me you will return for me. You must promise."

"Of course," he told her, feeling inexplicably sad.

Although he loathed the Electi in general, he was not entirely proud of having duped one so young and inexperienced.

"I promise," he said soberly, "And you must promise me that you will wait for me. We belong to each other now."

"Of course," she told him, smiling because she had echoed his very words. "Now go, Ryder. Quickly."

He kissed her again, but not on the lips — on the forehead. He had found that his ardor for her was only an adjunct to playing the game he had had to play to win her. Now that the match was over, she seemed almost distasteful to him. He couldn't wait to get away.

He turned and strode away, never looking back until he reached the shelter of the tree line. When he was far enough away that he could dare to, he flew toward the West. He started laughing to himself. Brynn, Warrior Queen, and Daughter of the Electi, was in for a shock. Gwenyth was a horny little fool that he refused to feel guilty about — she probably would have given it up for the first pimple-faced Warrior schoolboy from Natalia's school if he hadn't come along first. Definitely a hose hound, as hot as her older sister was cold.

Now that he was free, he wanted to bang his usual buxom tavern whores who knew their way around a man's body. He would be rich and beyond Brynn's reach. He was leaving, and he owed them nothing for all their haughty airs and disparaging looks.

Fuck the Electi, he thought, *fuck them all.*

CHAPTER THIRTEEN:
CURSE THE FATES

Natalia yelled out in utter frustration and anger, flipping the nearest table, and sending trinkets to shatter on the wooden floor beneath her bare feet.

"No," she shouted once more. "Seems fate has stepped in once more despite how strong my magic has become."

She said all of this to herself, as she preferred to practice her magic alone. Brynn hadn't known just how powerful she had become not only in the sciences they practiced furthering the race's survival, but in ritual as well. Except, when fate wanted something specific, it always got it no matter what was done to ensure a different outcome.

Natalia reached out and uttered one syllable, fire sparking to life in the very center of her outstretched palm. It burned, suspended in the still air just above her delicate flesh.

"Oh, destiny, I will not be beaten again."

Gwenyth slid through a crack in a seldom-used access door set into a corner of one of the stone-studded manse walls. It was fresh and dark as she slid in. Not even the guard paid much attention to this hidden door beneath its ivy bower, and she knew most of them had no idea that it existed — concealed as it was in the shadows of the climbing ivy and the overhanging trees.

To her right, she heard the shouting and bustle of the kitchen as the cooks prepared the evening meal. Instinctively, she turned away from that part of the passage and to the left, which seemed to dead end after about ten feet into a cupboard. She opened the door. It hadn't been opened for a while, and she made a face as the rusty hinges attached to the wooden door squealed in protest. Stooping, she got down on all fours and crawled into the dark space under the last shelf.

It was open, and she felt a draft as she crawled along for about five feet until it opened up again into a very narrow corridor that led to an even narrower circular staircase. As far as Gwenyth knew, she was the only inhabitant of the residence who knew this hidden staircase existed. She'd discovered it while exploring one day and nearly told Brynn about it. Then her older sister had pissed her off again and Gwenyth decided it would be her secret way in and out no matter how many of the Electi Guard Brynn assigned to keep her captive.

The staircase went up to the penthouse floor, and then back to Gwenyth's closet. Gwenyth suspected that there was a similar staircase on the opposite side of the front of the mansion that probably opened into the back of Brynn's closet. But one of the first things Brynn did after buying the estate was to have the older closet dry-walled in so she could create a room-sized walk-in closet within her large chamber. Gwenyth was offered the same renovation but refused. She loved the nuances of the old building with all of its strange passages and creaks. She also liked the idea that she could sneak out anytime she wanted to if she was careful.

Having reached the top of the stairs, Gwenyth pressed her shoulder to the wall to open the hidden door to the back of her closet. To her immense relief, it opened soundlessly, and she brushed past the couple rows of her clothing — mostly dresses mixed in with modern attire for outings — and opened the door into her room.

As soon as she did, she froze. Standing right in front of her not three feet away was Brynn, still in stained battle attire, and Bayn, looking agitated and perplexed at seeing her emerge from her closet. The two sisters stared at each other for a long moment. Gwenyth's mind raced as she tried to formulate some explanation for both her disheveled appearance and why she was inside her closet.

Brynn seemed to be sizing Gwenyth up, a look of suspicion on her beautiful face. Her crimson eyes were mere slits. Her eyes traveled down Gwenyth's body, at last coming to rest on Gwenyth's feet.

There was dried blood on the inside of both her younger sister's ankles.

Brynn opened her mouth and screamed.

"Well," Natalia said as she returned to her quarters at the school, and laid her large black leather medical bag on the granite counter underneath a row of test tubes. "That was rather unexpected."

"What, Natalia? Tell me. Everyone knows that something is going on. Lady Brynn was heard screaming less than an hour ago — and no one has *ever* heard her scream. Other than a war cry or something. You have to tell me what happened," her PA and apprentice Nellye said breathlessly, her huge brown eyes wide with curiosity.

Natalia turned back her hood, staring at the assistant contemplatively for a few moments. It was the kind of look Nellye had dubbed *the Natalia Stare*, and it seemed to pierce right through to her soul every time Natalia did it. After sighing deeply, Natalia relented.

"I cannot tell everything, but I can say this — the sanctity of the Princess Daughter of the Electi Gwenyth has been somewhat compromised. A part of her is missing."

Nellye gasped and covered her mouth.

"I knew that snotty little bitch was fucking Ryder Perkins. I came upon them one day in the labyrinth, and he had his head underneath her gown," the young woman said animatedly.

She knew Natalia was not overly fond of Gwenyth on a good day, so she felt she could comment freely. Natalia waggled a beautifully manicured finger in the air at her.

"No," she said, "Gwenyth is still technically a virgin. She has not lain with a male. If she had, she would have been forced into marriage with him immediately, as they would be considered husband and wife under Electi Law. No," she continued, "but she will probably be considered ruined all the same. Brynn has always had her work cut out for her as it is because of Gwenyth's withered arm. It is certainly a sad turn of events."

"And what of Ryder?" Nellye asked eagerly, "Is his head on a spike at Brynn's order?"

Natalia shook her head, amusement in her eyes.

"No. I am afraid he has deserted the Electi. Brynn is so bitter over it she will kill him on sight if she ever has the chance. Apparently, the story is spreading like wildfire."

"Oh yes, it is, High Oracle Natalia," Nellye said, her eyes still full of glee from being privy to the juiciest bit of gossip to fill the walls of the manse in years. "In fact, some of the young warriors were heard singing a rather derogatory song about the scandal."

This time Natalia's eyebrows raised in surprise.

"Really?" she said, genuinely surprised for the first time in a while. "What are they singing?"

"Well, if you don't mind my repeating it I can tell you," Nellye told her, looking around and closing one of the doors. "But you know our Warrior Leader Brynn would have my head for even repeating it. So listen carefully the first time," she joked.

The young woman cleared her throat and began to sing in a sweet voice that was high and clear.

Once a quiet afternoon
Where few words are spoken
Gwenyth lay on Ryder's knee
With her hymen broken
She shamed herself that very day
They hunted him, but he got away
Her reputation he did flay
Foolish Lady Gwenyth!

"That's the song they are singing," Nellye finished, looking pleased with herself.

"Catchy little tune, I think."

Terran leaned against the wall just outside Gwenyth's bedroom, his twin brother Bayn leaning just opposite of him. Terran heard Brynn's cry and came running as quickly as he could thinking the Liquidator chimera had done something to the Daughter of Electi, but no. Something more terrifying and scandalous had happened. Something none of them were prepared for. Gwenyth had never been one to cause trouble or even act out in response to her older sister's strict rules, but that had all changed. And it had all changed with Ryder Perkins.

"I knew that man was no good," Terran muttered, not even realizing he had spoken out loud until his brother's eyebrows rose in interest.

"Well, it seems your point was proven, brother. I'm sure you want to look Brynn in the eye and give her the big *I told you so speech*, huh?" Bayn answered with obvious irritation and anger in his voice even though it did not show on his face.

"No, I would never," Terran replied. Then a thought struck him. "Where were you two when this happened? Just before the battle was over you and Brynn were nowhere to be seen on the grounds. Where were you?"

He watched as Bayn lowered his eyes to the ground and a faint blush appeared on his cheeks, a small knowing smile spreading over his lips.

"Something happened, but it is private and really none of your business," Bayn answered as his face hardened at his brother's intrusive question.

"Did you," he paused and swallowed, not believing he was about to ask his brother this question. "Did you claim her?"

Silence for all of a moment, and then Bayn shook his head.

"No, I did not," he replied in a regretful tone.

"What do you mean?"

Bayn looked up at him, something in his face that Terran couldn't make out as his lips set in a straight line.

"She asked me to, but I didn't. I couldn't. It was as if something stopped our union, Terran, and I am not certain what to make of it."

Terran took a step forward but, just as he was about to open his mouth to shout at his brother for betraying him as well as to ask him about this force that got between the two of them, Brynn shot through Gwenyth's door. Tears streamed down her face as she stopped and registered the two large men standing in the hallway, apparently brimming with anger.

As soon as he saw her, Terran couldn't be angry with her, but he was going to speak to his brother once the entire scandal was over. Or as soon as they were alone again. But the urge to beat his brother to a bloody pulp was still ever present within him, slithering under his skin as an image of Brynn writhing beneath his twin came to the surface. He shook it off and turned to Brynn, knowing she would need both of them now more than ever.

"Brynn, is she alright?" Terran asked as he reached out to touch her shoulder.

As soon as his hand met her flesh he felt her shaking with despair and fury, her fists clenched at her sides as if she were trying to keep herself from throwing a punch at the first available person to cross her path.

"She is, for now. That is, until I get ahold of Ryder," she answered, her voice shaking with fury at every syllable.

Her eyes unfocused for a moment and then flicked to the stairs that would lead to the floor where her room was located. To where she was keeping Creed. Then she looked at Bayn.

"We'll need to talk," she said to him.

Bayn nodded as Terran shot him a look of pure rage.

"Alright." he pushed himself away from the wall.

Brynn put her hand out in a gesture telling him that he needed to stay put.

"Later. We will speak later. Right now, there is something I need to do."

With those words, she took off and took to the stairs, leaving them to wonder.

CHAPTER FOURTEEN:
NEEDED

Creed had heard the battle outside, and then the high feminine scream that he recognized as Brynn's. In a flurry of motion, he opened the door and attempted to leave the room he had been placed in. The Electi soldiers just outside his door stopped him as others all dressed in red came barreling down the hallway and up the nearly hidden staircase down the way.

Now, he was sitting in his room biting his nails and waiting to hear whether she was all right or not. Creed had found some clothes that fit him in the drawers and covered himself in a black cotton t-shirt and pants.

His leg bounced up and down with anxiety as the commotion finally ceased, and orders were shouted through the mansion. One name struck him multiple times.

205

Gwenyth. Something had happened to her, but he was perplexed as to what. He knew that since he had gone missing his father would most likely send a horde of Liquidators to collect him, and that they would kill a Daughter of Electi if they had the chance. He hoped that wasn't the case. He hopped up from the bed and shot toward the door.

"Fuck this," he muttered to himself.

Just as he approached the door, Brynn came bursting inside, her face covered in tears and black streaks from her mascara and eyeliner. It didn't matter to him that she was a mess. She was still beautiful, even if she was afraid. This was definitely a visit he hadn't expected after what had happened between them. Brynn still wore her blood-drenched clothing from where she had been bitten by the enchanted Hellhound, but now she was also coated in the black blood of the Liquidators. He smelled something else under the surface, a kind of male musk that wasn't his and had to stifle a growl of possession.

"Creed, I need your help," she said as she glanced at him and then began to pace, clenching and unclenching her fists as he watched her in abject terror.

"I heard you scream. Is everything okay?"

She stopped and stared at him, anger taking the place of fear on her face. Her crimson eyes stared daggers into him that nearly caused him to stumble backward as the cold wave of anger moved through his body.

"You fool, of course, it's not okay." She took a step toward him. "I'm going to kill him. I am going to kill Ryder Perkins as soon as I can get my eager hands on him."

"Ummm..." was all he knew to say.

"He took something that did not belong to him, Creed. Now she is bound to him for as long as he breathes, and I need your help in making certain those breaths stop. Can you help me, Creed?"

Creed placed his hands on her slender shoulders and bent down slightly to look evenly into her eyes.

"Brynn, what are you talking about, love?"

She took a deep and shuddering breath to steady herself.

"Ryder has taken her purity and ran off. I believe I know who he is working for, but I am not certain, and I *will* see him dead."

Creed's eyebrows stitched together in utter confusion.

"Who do you believe he works for, Brynn? How can I possibly help you?"

"I believe he is working for your father, Creed, and you will help me gain the information I need to find him. You can move among them, and I will have your back at a moment's notice. I couldn't think of anyone else to come to because, if the entire House of Electi kicks in their doors, we can be certain they will move in on my house and kill everyone inside our ranks, moving from house to house to exterminate us all. That has been their ultimate goal since creation, but I will see to it that they do not reach their aim."

"You're rambling on, Brynn."

Creed backed away from her and ran his hand through his hair and down his face as he sat on the corner of the bed.

She shook her head and continued, "You will help me find out where Ryder Perkins is, and you will take me with you. I want him kneeling before me. I want him to fall to my blade."

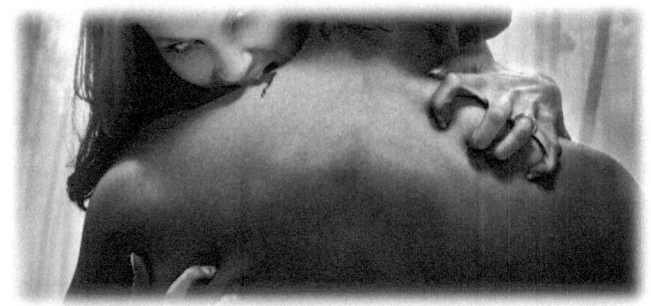

CHAPTER FIFTEEN:
INTERROGATION & BATTLE WOUNDS

Brynn had changed her clothes as quickly as possible, washed the dried blood from her body, and stole some pieces from Bayn and Terran for Creed. Seeing as they were relatively the same size she had a feeling that their boots and pants would fit alright. Sneaking past the others would be easy enough, using the back stairway that she had caught Gwenyth using after her unholy tryst with Ryder Perkins. She didn't need any of them trying to talk her out of her current course of action. She would find her answers and then come back to collect them for the finale.

She didn't need the grief of taking their prisoner out where he could either harm her or escape, but she trusted him. She wasn't even sure why. Was it the vision Leo spoke of? Brynn shook the questions away and continued to walk beside Creed.

Now, Brynn and Creed were striding in downtown Los Angeles, looking for the club that Creed had stated was an underground for the Liquidators. A place where those like her weren't just meant for death, but were slaves up until that moment, so they learned who the true masters of the human race were. The pair weaved through the people, no one paying attention to them in the night while they hustled to their destinations.

Creed had informed her of how she was supposed to act once they entered the club. Subservient, docile even, but she doubted she could act such a way when surrounded by her ultimate enemy. Especially when some may recognize her as the eldest Daughter of the Electi. Their ruler, their leader, and enemy number one.

She turned her head to look at him while still weaving flawlessly through the throng.

"So, Creed, what is the name of this place again?" she asked him, her voice higher pitched than usual from the anxiety she felt roiling within her gut.

"The Underground, Daughter of Electi," Creed replied with a smirk.

"How appropriate," she said with a nod.

Creed laughed that quiet, melodic laugh that made her insides tighten. As if her body wasn't already tense enough. She was dressed to the nines in a skimpy black dress that hugged every curve of her body and knee-high black leather boots to match. She had hidden a blade within the very top of her boots, and the sword she usually loved to carry was unceremoniously left at home. The small blade, as well as a small handgun tucked into the other boot, were her only weapons. She hated not having her precious sword on her, and she detested firearms, but it would have to do. She just hoped she had hidden them well enough to keep them from being taken at the door.

"Yes, I guess you could say that." He looked over at her and frowned. "There's something we have to do before we get there. It's right down the block underneath Exchange LA."

"Underneath?" Brynn asked with a note of skepticism in her voice.

"Yes, Brynn, underneath. The owner of Exchange is one of us and has managed to keep the Underground a secret since the business started."

Brynn nodded in understanding. "And what is it we have to do before we get there?"

Without warning, Creed's massive hand wrapped around her wrist and pulled her to the side toward a dank and dark alley, deep within the shadows so they couldn't be seen. He pushed her against the building's exterior, the brick rough on her exposed shoulders, and pressed his body against hers.

"Creed?" she yelped. "What the fuck?"

She felt his erection press up against her belly and had to force herself not to look away from his beautiful eyes. She had grown to trust him, but not completely, and this sudden action surprised her. Her mind went instantly to where her weapons were as her body responded to him in the only way she couldn't control.

"You do not have to fear me, Daughter of Electi." He took a deep breath in like he smelled her as they stood in such proximity and then sighed. "You are known for being the beauty of the vampire world, Brynn. That and those crimson eyes... the color of blood. I am confident they will not recognize your face, but with those red beauties, you can bet that someone will notice."

"Oh," she muttered, "what do you suggest we do? It's a little too late to do anything about it now. And the *Sapphire Eye* isn't exactly helpful even if I could control it."

"Oh how right you are, but I believe I can be of some assistance. Now, close your eyes."

She stared up at him incredulously, studying him as his body reacted to his closeness against her. Her eyes narrowed to slits under his stare, causing him to sigh in frustration and shake his head.

"Goddammit, Brynn. Just do it. Haven't I proven I won't harm you in any way?"

As she stared up at him, she knew it to be true, but he was part Liquidator. A chimera mixed with vampire and angel as well. The darkness of the Liquidator part of him still lingered inside of him. The look in his eyes and the way his body pressed hers to the exterior of the building in all the right places, caused her to drop her guard slightly, her shoulders sagging in submission.

"I guess you're right." She slowly closed her eyes.

"That's my girl," Creed said.

Then she felt the tips of his fingers rest just over her eyelids with just enough pressure that she could barely sense his touch. Her eyes tingled slightly right around her pupils and then his touch vanished along with the sensation. She opened her eyes, and he smiled down at her, pleased with himself it seemed.

"There she is, and with a new pair of eyes. Now," he pulled away from her and reached his hand out to her. "How about we go dancing?"

Brynn beamed at the silly request and took his hand.

Creed's body still reacted to being so close to Brynn as they walked the rest of the way to the Liquidator's club, their haven within the city. As soon as the man at the door recognized who he was, it was as easy as ever to gain entry into the dance club above ground, and then through to the Underground below the loud music and grinding bodies on the dance floor. Of course, it couldn't rival the sexual tension within the Liquidator's lair just beneath. You wouldn't only see dancing, but even intercourse took place out in the open. Nothing to hide and no one could care less.

The music upstairs was stupid, pop music remixed to dubstep, but downstairs they at least had good taste. Once they were down the stairs, Brynn followed just as he had instructed her to while there, Panic! At the Disco's *Miss Jackson* pumped through the speakers as a bottle of Grey Goose vodka made its rounds on the dance floor.

Creed turned, looked at Brynn, and cringed when he saw her, never wanting to see her in a subservient manner. She was beautiful, strong, and courageous. Not this weak little thing that let men tower over her. His heart ached even though he knew it was necessary. He leaned down to her so she could hear him, pressing his lips to her ear.

"Stay close to me, alright? Liquidator males are known to just snatch a pretty little thing like you up without a care as to who she belongs to. There are vampire servants in the place, but they will not help you even if they recognize you. Do you understand?"

Her eyes, now a vibrant violet in color, flicked up to his face and back down to the floor.

"Yes, I understand."

"Good," he responded with a nod.

Creed pushed through the crowd and felt Brynn sticking close to his back as he moved, pushing through anyone who got in his way. A few had realized who he was and parted like the Red Sea. A few weren't even paying attention, already drunk beyond comprehension. He knew who he was looking for. As soon as he approached the bar, he leaned over it and placed his elbows on the countertop lit up with blue LED lights. The bartender came to him right away with a white rag in his hands.

"I need to speak to Kade." When the bartender barely moved, he put more force into his voice. "Now."

"Yes, Commander," the slight man said as he moved out from behind the bar.

Creed looked back at Brynn as he began to follow and jerked his head toward their destination, a back room within the Underground where Kade remained and watched those in his sights to stop any trouble that may start quickly. She followed without having to be asked. Creed had to admit she was a great actress, and even more beautiful than those that graced the silver screen.

In what felt like seconds, they stood in front of the reinforced steel door that led to Kade's office. The bartender moved out of the way so Creed could enter his credentials. As the son of their leader, he was allowed access anywhere he desired. Kade's office was no exception.

Once he entered the eight-digit passcode into the keys on the outside of the door, it sprung open and allowed them entry into Kade's office. Both of them stepped through and the door swung closed at Brynn's back. She still clung to Creed as instructed.

Creed was the first to spot Kade. The tall man was dressed in an expensive gray pin-stripe suit and dress shirt open at the collar, his shining dress shoes reflecting the lights coming through the large pane of the two-way mirror as he stood in front of it and watched those on the dance floor. He turned, his black hair slicked back, and his bright green eyes studied them before he smiled.

"Creed, son of our King, what brings you to the Underground?" He peered around Creed and noticed Brynn there, eyes averted to the floor with her back straight. "And who is this beauty?"

Creed glanced over his shoulder at Brynn who hadn't moved an inch since they entered the room.

"She is not why I am here, Kade." Creed looked back to the man in front of him. "I need your help."

Kade's eyebrows raised in interest as he moved away from the glass to sit down in a plush, round chair five feet away. A lit cigar smoked in the ashtray on the glass table beside him along with a glass of what Creed could tell was scotch. Kade picked up the cigar and placed it between his lips, taking a drag. A ring of smoke left from between those same lips as he pulled it away.

"You? Need my help, Creed? And since when did you take a slave?"

Creed shook his head and ignored the second question.

"Yes, I need your help. Do you know of

someone by the name of Ryder Perkins? A vampire working for my father within the Electi ranks."

Kade's head bobbed as he took another drag from the cigar, blowing out beautifully fragrant smoke.

"Yes, I do. What has he done?"

"This stays in this room, Kade, do you understand?"

"I do, my liege. I do."

Creed relaxed enough to move to the massive leather couch positioned across from where Kade sat, taking a seat. He patted the cushion next to him, and Brynn followed blindly, taking her place beside him as a slave would. He had to fight the urge to tell her to stop. Kade's eyes never left Brynn as she moved, and he had to fight the streak of urgent jealousy that struck through him.

Clearing his throat, he began.

"The Electi took me prisoner and, instead of doing his job, he got what he came for and left me to die. I want revenge. That's where you come in."

Kade glanced at Creed for a second and studied Brynn again.

"How can I help you?"

"I want you to tell me where he is headed. I know you know or, if you don't, you are aware of someone who does."

Creed's heart pounded rapidly as the question hung in the air between them, making him anxious as he waited. Uncomfortably, Brynn shifted under Kade's gaze and moved closer to Creed so her thigh brushed his. Kade continued to scan her as if undressing her with his eyes. That filled Creed with rage, but he swallowed it down long enough to wait for his reply.

"He is going to the only place he can at this point with what he was drafted to take from the Electi, Creed. You know full well where that is."

Brynn's breathing picked up a beat, but he did his best to ignore it. Kade just continued to stare.

"Shit, Kade. Then it looks like I'm going to my father's, and you know how much he hates even having to look at me," Creed said as he stood from the couch.

What he said wasn't a lie. His father hated having to look him in the eye because he reminded him so much of his deceased mother. Creed understood it on some level but so desperately needed the love of his father and the acknowledgment of his presence. Creed snapped his fingers and Brynn was at his side in an instant. Kade came to stand before them, strolling in their direction as he stared even more intensely at Brynn. This made Creed even more nervous. Kade stuffed one hand into his pocket and puffed the cigar again.

They were about to make their way out as soon as Creed swung the door open, but Kade took Brynn's wrist in his free hand and spoke with the cigar placed between his lips.

"You seem to have gotten yourself an

218

Electi slave, haven't you, dear Prince," he said in more of a statement than a question. "An exquisite one at that."

Brynn flinched and attempted to jerk her hand away from him, but failed as he pulled her closer to him. He looked her directly in the eye, taking in the violet hue. There was nothing Creed could do to stop him except one thing.

"She is not your property, Kade. She is mine, and you'd do better to remember that."

A wave of energy passed over the entire club. Brynn stumbled a step and shook her head as if ridding herself of horrible images, her eyes closed. When they popped open, they were bright crimson and flashed the bright Sapphire blue under Kade's magic.

"Oh, this one is the property of no one," Kade snarled.

Brynn's breath caught in her throat as the words left the man's mouth, alarm bells going off inside her mind as the man opened his mouth and yelled above the music.

"Electi," he shouted, reaching around to his back, and pulling out a large pistol.

Everyone outside the office scattered, screams and shrieks coming from all directions. Brynn kicked out at the man, causing him to fall to one knee. When she punched him, he dropped the gun to the floor. It skittered across the ground, and she turned to find Creed there, standing in the threshold of the office with his hand out to her.

"Let's get the fuck out of here," he yelled above the chaos.

She took it without question, and they ran through the Underground together, able to make it past everyone and up into the human club — the only exit. Gunshots rang out from the stairs that led down to the Underground. A bullet whizzed past Brynn and barely missed her outstretched arm as Creed ran with her behind him.

The humans inside the club upstairs screamed and ran toward the exit. There was no way Brynn and Creed could blend into that crowd. That much she knew. The flashing lights around her only caused her eyes to flicker from red to blue only to settle on the glowing blue she was known for because of her gift. A gift everyone, even the Liquidators, knew was exclusive to her and her alone. Brynn pulled on Creed's arm, and he turned to her as they froze in the middle of the dance floor, the humans running around them until there were only a few stragglers, gunfire erupting into the club as the Liquidators moved in.

"They want a war, let's give them what they're looking for," Brynn shouted over the thump of the music around them that moved through her entire body.

Creed nodded.

Brynn reached down into her right boot and gripped the pistol she had placed there, bringing it out, raising it up, and turning off the safety in one swift move as Creed reached into the folds of his long coat and removed two larger handguns from within. She pulled the trigger, the recoil barely registering in her vibrant muscles as the bullet passed through the air and hit the first Liquidator between the eyes.

She reached into the other bootleg and pulled out a switchblade, revealing its silver blade with a flourish. At least six large men came to surround them. When she spotted Creed, he had his pistols out and aimed out to the sides to hit any that came at them from either direction. They looked at each other again and nodded.

The Liquidators, all dressed in expensive black suits, descended on them at that moment. Brynn only had one magazine with six rounds in it, so she knew she had to make sure every shot counted or not use it at all. She opted for hand-to-hand with the blade unless the pistol was necessary.

She slashed out at the first man to greet her blade, slicing down. The blade glided through flesh, and a straight line appeared down the center of the man's face, black blood seeping out of it as rage boiled inside the Liquidator's muscles. He came back at her, and she aimed the gun dead center, taking him out with one shot. He fell to the ground at her feet, the entry wound smoking slightly from the close-range kill.

Creed used his guns to the fullest

extent. His were much larger and carried more rounds because he had a better place to hide them. As she exchanged blows and swipes with a Liquidator who was as pale as she was, she caught his movements out of the corner of her eye. Creed was lithe, sleek, and deadly, taking no time at all to dispatch the three that had come in his direction. The coat billowed around him beautifully, and she could not deny her attraction to him then. Not even from those she knew.

A punch landed at her temple, causing her ears to ring as she fell to the ground. She jumped up quickly and twirled her blade in her hand, throwing it toward the Liquidator's head. Her aim was perfect, the blade catching him in the center of his forehead. Black blood oozed out around the silver blade as he slumped to a heap on the ground.

The war cry of one last Liquidator rang out over the thumping music as Brynn noticed not a single human being was left in the building. She turned, raised her gun, and aimed it at the Liquidator that was now only a couple feet from her. She saw Creed just past him do the same. They both took aim at the Liquidator's head and fired. As soon as the body dropped to the floor, Creed shoved his guns back into the folds of his coat and the pockets within them, and was on her, his lips crashing down on hers in an embrace of passion and adrenaline. Lust so intense it caused her to ache ran through her in an instant.

Shouts came as more Liquidators moved up the stairs from the Underground, and they poured into Exchange.

"As I said before... let's get the fuck out of here," Creed said as he pulled away from her and took her hand in his.

"Absolutely."

They ran out of Exchange, dodging startled bystanders outside the building as gunshots rang out and missed them every time. Once they were confident they had lost them, Creed's hand took hold of her wrist, and he pulled her deep into an alley, pushing her up against the wall again. He kissed her feverishly. Even though she was still a virgin, lust ran through her. White hot and inescapable. She sure as Hell didn't mind losing her purity to him in that instant.

She kissed him back, her hands moving underneath his shirt and raking down his chest. He growled against her lips and reached beneath her short skirt. His fingers grazed the wet fabric, and he growled again, nibbling at her neck as he pulled at the thong she wore, tearing it from her body.

Brynn reached down and unzipped his pants as his erection pushed seemingly painfully against his fly. It sprang free, and she gripped him, moving her hand up and down to pleasure him. She writhed against him, her body doing what it knew it needed to. She had no experience with men, but her instincts drove her. Her body was alight with excitement and she breathed heavily, Creed alternating from groaning, kissing, and biting. She licked his earlobe and placed her lips next to his ear.

"Take me, Creed. Claim me. Right here. Right now," she whispered.

He pulled back slightly and looked her in the eyes, happiness, lust, and worry crossing over his features.

"It will be painful, are you certain?" he asked, panting as she continued to pleasure him with her hand.

"Yes," she said without taking her eyes off him.

She loved that he didn't have to be told twice. He gripped her thighs just below her ass and hoisted her up and, without wasting a single second, thrust into her. Pain assaulted her senses at first and caused her to cry out, but was replaced quickly with pleasure as he moved inside of her. Their bodies flooded with ecstasy as they rode the waves together, each moan and sigh causing them to ride even higher with each stroke.

It didn't take long before a wave of pulse-pounding pleasure rocked them both and Brynn's body pulsated around him, drawing him deeper. He shuddered against her as he nipped at her collarbone. They came together, and he cradled her there, but it wasn't long enough before he pulled back and looked her in the eyes, pushing strands of soaked blonde and red hair from her face. He opened his mouth and said three words she hadn't expected to hear from a man.

"I love you," he panted.

She planted a chaste kiss on his lips and answered, "I love you."

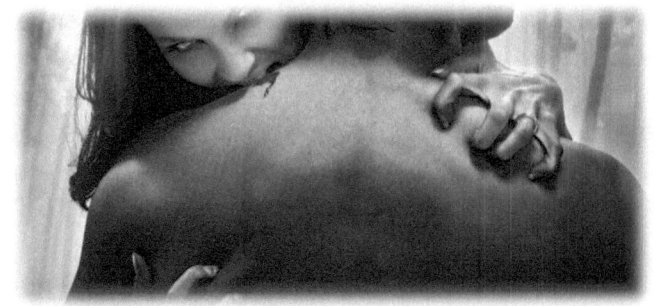

CHAPTER SIXTEEN:
CHOSEN

The House of Electi was in utter chaos as everyone searched the mansion for both Creed and Brynn, having no indication they would both take off after the revelation that Gwenyth had given herself to a traitor.

Gwenyth sat in the living room curled up in blankets and watched the hustle and bustle, Calyx shouting orders as second in command.

"Where the Hell is she? She can't have just disappeared. Find them," she yelled once more as she came into the living room and stared at Gwenyth. She placed her hands on her hips. "Are you certain she didn't speak a word to you? She didn't mention taking off?"

Gwenyth nodded her head and pulled the blanket around her even tighter, feeling the chill of Calyx's hard gaze move over her flesh.

"No, Calyx, she didn't speak a word. She

just sat there in silence and stared at the wall. Then she got up and left. I am sorry."

Calyx sighed and let her shoulders sag, moving to sit beside the younger Daughter of Electi.

"No, it is I who am sorry, Gwenyth."

"For what?"

"Not being able to see that he was a traitor before all of this happened," she said as she waved her hand around to indicate that she was talking about the past week's events. "If I had paid more attention I could have stopped him before he did this to you."

"No one knew, Calyx. Please don't blame yourself," she said as she reached out toward Calyx, interrupted from the gesture by Bayn and Terran coming into the room like raging bulls.

"She is nowhere, Calyx. Is it time to call Natalia?"

Calyx nodded and stood, "Yes, bring the Oracle. We don't have time to waste."

As soon as the words left her mouth, there was a loud sound as the front doors of the mansion groaned open. Those who had once been running about in search of their leader stopped in their tracks, frozen in place. Bayn and Terran turned toward the sound, but Gwenyth couldn't see anything. She stood, dropped her blanket to the floor, and walked around the two large men. What she spotted in the doorway made her gasp, her hand rising to her lips to stifle the sound.

Brynn and Creed stood there,

surrounded in moonlight like an apparition.

"Is it her?" Calyx asked as she came to stand beside Gwenyth, placing protective hands on her thin shoulders. "Oh my God, Brynn?"

Gwenyth looked on in shock as her sister and the Chimera stood in the doorway. Brynn took a step forward, and a scent that was unmistakable moved through the air. Musk, lilies, and sex wafted toward her nostrils, and she knew it had happened. Her sister had been mated with the Liquidator, and everyone knew it. There was no denying it.

"What the fuck did you do to her, Liquidator?" Bayn growled as he took a protective step forward, the rage in him causing the scent of soot and fire to clash with Brynn's scent.

"Nothing she didn't want, vampire," Creed barked back.

Bayn bucked up toward the large male, possession, and a territorial urge caused both of them to ripple with anger and pent-up energy.

"Enough," Brynn shouted. She looked at Bayn with so much rage the room went cold. "We will discuss this at another time. Do you understand me?"

Gwenyth watched in silence as Bayn's eyes filled with jealous rage, but he nodded and did as her older sister asked without question. He took a few steps back from Creed and leaned against the wall.

"Now," Brynn started as she

straightened and pushed her hair away from her face and off of her shoulders, "I know where that bastard is headed. Who will come with me to see that justice is dealt?"

As exhausted as they all were from the battle, they knew their Warrior Queen Brynn was not waiting for Ryder Perkins to get any further away. Wearily, they all quickly showered and changed their soiled clothing to fresh battle attire, drank blood to renew and refresh their immortal bodies, and gathered in the Grand Hall before the East door.

Brynn came bursting across the room from the freight elevator, her long hair flowing behind her, followed by a resolute-looking Calyx.

"Brynn," Tarren said stepping so that he was in front of her, and unzipping the diagonal zipper that went from shoulder to his pectoral that he'd had sewn specifically in his sweater so that Brynn could feed from him easily. "Do you need to feed? I am, as always, at your service."

Brynn looked at him but seemed to look past him.

"Thank you. I already have, Tarren," she said brusquely.

For a moment, color shone high on her cheekbones as she remembered the same offer just minutes beforehand from Creed — that had been the offer that she could not refuse.

Not only did she desire for her formidable skills to be at their best, but also she found that his blood had amazing effects on her in other ways.

Their private exchange a few minutes earlier had had but one witness — Calyx. Calyx understood the necessity of using every advantage available to them to protect their kingdom and their people. She had turned her back at Brynn's request, as Brynn had sunk her fangs for the second time into the hollow of Creed's throat. It was more than a mere feeding, and both of them knew it. Creed had pushed his immense erection against her as she fed, and she had fed ferociously, the points of her nipples hard as diamonds. The arousal she felt feeding on this giant of a male creature was as incredible as it was inexplicable.

Just as she had finished feeding she reached down for a moment and captured the immense crown of his cock between her dainty thumb and index fingers as they exchanged a look so smoldering that the air between them crackled with static electricity. Then Brynn was all hard edges and battle-driven, focused on the only thing that mattered above all else.

Revenge.

Tarren nodded his head at Brynn's rebuff, confused. His confusion was immediately replaced by the fury of realizing that the hostage Creed had replaced him.

By a mongrel angel. A *fucking* angel.

Brynn had one of the Elite Guard unfold

a map and spread it on the flagstones.

"I am almost sure he is headed to Crimayne," Brynn told them. "Since he has a head start, we will need to head him off somehow before he ever reaches their mansion."

Everyone present was silent, studying the map. No one wanted to tell Brynn that they had almost zero chance of heading Ryder off at that point. A journey to Crimayne might take a few hours, but he had a good enough start so that even if he ran, rather than flying all the way he could easily elude their Tracking Party.

Calyx spoke up in answer to their baffled expressions.

"I know of a portal that will take us to Canyon Run, the part of the mountain on the opposite side of their stead. From there we can lie in wait for him and bide our time. I also feel that we are expected. Natalia tells me that the Liquidators have their own Seers and Oracles, and one is a particularly nasty Wraith. We will have to be careful as we travel through town because they might know we are coming and send a War party of their own to head us off."

Calyx looked at Brynn, her expression filled with concern.

"I think you should stay behind and let the rest of us take care of Ryder, Brynn. I am afraid for you although I cannot tell you why. If I promise to bring you his severed head, will you stay here?"

Brynn started to reject Calyx's plea

outright, but softened her tone when she saw the fear in Calyx's eyes.

"My Warrior Sister, you know I cannot," she answered. "The honor of the House of Electi rests on what we do next. We must prevail. Now that the traitor has been flushed from our midst, we must hunt him down and kill him like the animal he is. Anyway," she continued, "I have a bargaining chip."

As if on cue, the freight elevator came to life, resting at last on the East side of the sub-basement floor with a metallic groan. Everyone's attention was riveted as the massive freight doors slowly opened.

Standing in the doorway of the industrial elevator, his muscles rippling through his black t-shirt and his long leather coat blowing in the slight breeze was Creed. Everyone watched him as he strode forward, his air of confidence unmistakable. He made a commanding figure with his stature, his delineated muscles, and his noble bearing. Tarren scowled darkly, his eyes flashing under hooded lids, though he said nothing. Bayn had a different reaction entirely.

The most recent event hit him hard. He was aware that Creed had claimed the only female he had ever loved, and the anguish ripped through his heart at that relived moment of recognition. It was, by far, the most painful sensation he had ever experienced. Unlike the battle wounds he had endured, as deep as some of them were. The recent recognition that another male had claimed

Brynn was the deepest cut of all.

"Stop staring, all of you," Brynn said mockingly. "How oddly you are behaving. Stop playing statues and get ready to head out. We will be riding to the portal in the Electi's designated vehicles so we can save our energy. Creed and I will take the lead. Tarren and Bayn, you can bring up the rear."

Everyone nodded and then exited. A half-circle of the finest cars on the property were parked outside. As they climbed inside, several of the Electi Royal Guard joined them. The sun had nearly set, and a silver crescent of a moon became visible against the deepening azure of the evening sky.

Brynn's hair shone silver in the light of the moon and stars. As she sat behind the wheel with her window open, she appeared more beautiful than ever.

Even Calyx was startled by Brynn's appearance, but then she knew.

Brynn, Warrior Queen, and Daughter of the Electi had at last found love.

CHAPTER SEVENTEEN:
VENGEANCE IS BEST SERVED COLD

They rode hard to the West, and then the East for a bit as the moon climbed higher in the sky. At last, Calyx sent Brynn a text message, signaling them to turn onto a back road that they sped down with due haste. They all found themselves in a tree-ringed clearing, parking in front of what seemed to be a tunnel formed from the branches of long dead trees, leaning inward toward each other from opposite sides to create what appeared to be an entrance.

Calyx slipped out of her car and slid out into the cool night air, her eyes sparkling with excitement. She began humming, a pleasant and somewhat monotonous sound that increased in volume. The rest of the group exited their vehicles and stood silently, assuming Calyx was calling upon some ancient magic of the Fae Folk.

Fireflies gathered around the entrance of the tunnel before them, the soft glow of their twinkling lights increasing in brightness around the dark entrance until it was visible. Calyx seemed to be in her element. She turned around to the others excitedly.

"They don't come unless the portal is stable," she said, smiling. "So we can be sure it is. We should end up on the back side of Crimayne when we reach the other side, making a nice shortcut, saving us hours, and enabling us to catch that despicable Ryder before he even reaches the Liquidator King Uictore."

Tarren chose that moment to get a dig in at Creed.

"So, son of Uictore, King of the Liquidators — how does it feel to be home again?" he asked, a snide tone in his voice.

"Not my favorite, actually," Creed answered him, looking straight ahead at the entrance to the portal. A faint glimmer of light came from way back in the darkness and grew brighter and closer. "And this has not been my home since I was little more than a child, you asshole."

Tarren moved toward Creed, his fists clenched, aching to connect his massive fist with Creed's too handsome face. To his chagrin, Brynn placed herself immediately between them.

"Tarren," she said coldly, staring him down, "You forget yourself. As long as I have accepted Creed and vouchsafed for him, you must treat him with respect. I will tolerate nothing less. Do we understand each other?"

Tarren lowered his fist, but his fingers still twitched at his side. Nevertheless, he bowed his head in deference to his Ruler.

"It shall be as you say, Brynn, Daughter of the Electi," he expressed in an even tone he could barely manage.

Inwardly Brynn fumed. What she really wanted was to have Tarren bend over so she could kick him in the ass. Just when she needed the Twins to be playing their A-game they were both being assholes.

Overhead, a shadow passed over them briefly.

"Fuck," Calyx said, surprising them.

To Brynn's questioning look, she quickly explained.

"I think that was Ryder passing over us just now. I know he didn't see us because of the overhang of the trees, but I am fairly sure it was him."

"Fine," Brynn said, pulling her favorite sword out of its sheath and unbuckling her utility belt that held an array of weapons before letting it fall to the ground. "I am going after him. He will never live to reach Crimayne."

Without another word, she took off, moving upward at a high velocity. Her war cries drifted back down to them. Tarren and Bayne immediately followed suit. The only ones remaining of the Royal Entourage, Calyx, and Creed, eyeballed each other warily.

"Why aren't you joining her?" Creed asked Calyx, a twinkle in his eye.

"I am staying to guard you," Calyx said, amused. "I still distrust you, Creed, even though Brynn vouches for you. Why aren't you following her?"

Creed chuckled.

"Because Brynn has got this. By the time I could get up there, if I could get up there, he'd be dead. My flying skills are a bit rusty."

As if on cue, hearing the rushing sound above them of an object plummeting to earth, both Creed and Calyx stepped back from where they had been standing. Almost immediately, an object hit the ground between them.

Ryder's severed head.

His body soon followed. Calyx cast her eyes upward, but did not see Brynn yet. She busied herself checking the pockets of Ryder's blood-saturated jacket while Creed watched. He saw her dart a hand inside Ryder's tunic, to an inside pocket, and he saw her smile, her eyes gleaming as she retrieved a folded white kerchief.

"They shall not have you, Gwenyth," he heard her murmur. "They shall not have you, oh, Daughter of the Electi."

Calyx placed the kerchief tenderly into the suede bag at her waist, patting it for good measure. When she looked up again, her eyes met Creeds.

"I'm sure there is a story in there somewhere," he remarked, gesturing at the drawstring bag at Calyx's waist.

"Yes, there is," Calyx assured him. "Not one you'll hear from my lips, Liquidator. Brynn may tell it to you. That is her privilege if she so desires, but I don't trust you."

Creed frowned, holding his hands out in a placating gesture.

"Have I offended you in some way that I can help?" Creed asked. "I cannot help my lineage, though I imagine you spit on Chimeras when you come across them. I cannot help that three different rivers of blood course through these veins of mine, but I assure you that I would protect Brynn's immortal body with my own, even if it costs me everything. Calyx, I know you can tell if I am lying. Surely you know I speak the truth."

Calyx stared at him for what seemed an eternity and then replied in a voice deeper than the one she usually used.

"It is not her body that I fear you will bring to harm, Mongrel," she answered, seeming to look past him, "but rather her heart."

At that moment, Brynn returned, Bayn and Tarren at her heels smiling.

"You should have seen our Warrior Queen," Tarren said. There was nothing he loved more than seeing Brynn ace a kill. "One stroke. He never got a word out."

"Ended," Bayn chimed in. "Magnificent."

Brynn, ignoring the accolades, trotted

over to where Ryder's head lay face up, a shocked expression on his face. She picked him up by the hair and held his head facing her at eye level.

"I have ended your perfidy," she said, talking to him as if he could still hear her, "Now they will sing a different song when I display your severed head on a spike from my balcony. They will sing of the crows feasting on your eyes and lying tongue. And I, Brynn, daughter of the Electi, will sing the loudest."

After an awkward moment's silence, her crimson eyes flashed a sapphire blue in the darkness. She blushed with embarrassment as her companions watched her with wide eyes.

"And we will meet his master."

It was not far from Crimayne. Brynn and her band had headed Ryder off just in time. Her deep satisfaction at removing his despicable head from his shoulders had reenergized her, and she couldn't wait to meet Uictore *The Vanquisher*, face to face. As they got within several yards, Creed caught up with Brynn to depart what he considered vital information.

"I don't think a frontal assault is our best choice, Daughter of the Electi, although I know you have no fear. I believe we can spare some casualties by using the element of surprise."

"Isn't showing up completely unexpected enough of a surprise?" she retorted impatiently. "If you have a suggestion, state it quickly because I am still thirsty for Liquidator blood."

"This way," Creed said immediately, motioning to the others.

Crimayne was oddly built, both for a mansion or any other massive structure. Modeled after Predjamski Grad, a Slovenian castle whose name literally meant *Castle in front of a cave*. It was protected on the back side by the mountain it was butted up against. The huge mansion continued into the cavernous opening into the mountain. Though a third of it adjoined the mountain, there were only low stone walls that ran along the sides. Brynn and her warriors quickly scaled them and continued to one side of the structure.

"I don't see any doors," she said to Creed as he flanked her.

"Oh, they are there," he assured her, his lips twisting upward into a grin. "I assure you. I used to sneak in and out at will when I was a boy. You will soon see what I am talking about."

So far, they had seen no one and heard no alerts sounding to indicate they'd been spotted. Creed walked right up to the stone studded outside wall of the structure and stood a moment, rubbing his chin.

"Well?" Brynn said impatiently, watching him.

"Hold up," he said, immediately

241

dropping to his knees and running his long fingers along the bottom of one wall. After a few seconds, he said, "Aha."

He held up his hand. In it was a long, ornately fashioned silver key.

Everyone stood back. The twins, silently taking in Creed's movements, still did not completely trust him not to turn on Brynn. Calyx moved imperceptibly closer to Brynn to protect her if she were attacked. Creed turned for a moment, sensing that they were positioning themselves in case they needed to take him out.

"Paranoid much?" he asked.

He chuckled under his breath as he inserted the key into a keyhole that was part of a dark fissure running across the stone wall.

It must be on springs, Brynn thought to herself as the huge door opened outward smoothly and soundlessly.

Creed poked his head in. It was completely dark within the opening, and Calyx wordlessly handed him a small high-powered flashlight. She then pulled out a Green laser grid light from her pocket and switched it on. Between the two of them, they would not only be able to detect the presence of another Earthly entity, but also detect the Shadow Demons that were known to be minions for the Liquidator King.

They proceeded cautiously. The opening itself was wide enough for them to enter two abreast and the ceilings were high enough so that even the tallest of them, Creed, Tarren, and Bayn, were able to walk upright without hitting their heads. Creed abruptly turned around after they had gone a few yards, with the corridor leading upwards, and addressed the group.

"This passage culminates in a door just off the Reception Chamber," he told them. "That probably means you are about to meet my Father, Uictore. I have no idea what his reaction will be seeing me again. And as for the rest of you — Brynn, Daughter of the Electi, I have no idea if the Liquidator King is still abiding by the Accords of the Interdimensional Alliance of 1514 or not. When I left, he was — meaning he will not kill you on sight even if you are trespassing. But I do know one thing. He is not overly fond of Fairies," Creed finished, throwing a significant look in Calyx's direction.

"I don't care what his preferences are," Brynn answered, pushing past Creed.

As she did, she felt his hands resting, unseen and momentarily on the small of her back and over the swell of her buttocks. She thought it bold of him, but smiled to herself, remembering for a moment the pounding swell of him inside her.

When she heaved the door to the Reception room open, she saw a stout velvet curtain in front of her. She cast it roughly aside to enter the chamber. The others in her Royal entourage followed, the rest hanging back in case they were needed and per her

243

instructions, still concealed by the burgundy velvet curtains.

The huge, bearded man wearing a crown fashioned of the fangs of his enemies turned and smiled at her. Brynn was surprised. All of the descriptions she had ever heard of the Liquidator King did not match the benevolent-looking being she saw several feet before her. His Guard flanked him and on the opposite side, there was a woman who was at least six feet tall, raven-haired, and built like a huntress. She could have been Natalia's twin, she looked so much like her.

The male figure on the throne gestured them forward.

"Please, Warrior Queen Brynn, Daughter of the Electi, come around front here so that I don't get a crick in my neck. Welcome to Crimayne, the most glorious fortress of a castle in the third plane of existence. We have been expecting you."

Brynn proceeded with dignity, Bayn, Tarren, Creed, Calyx, and the others following her. Her heart pounded and her mind raced with confusion. How could it be that they had been expected?

Uictore continued to stare at Brynn.

"You are every bit as beautiful as you are purported to be, Oh Daughter of the Electi," he said slowly. He looked her up and down in a way that made her uncomfortable, letting his eyes linger on the tops of her full breasts displayed proudly at the top of her leather battle corset. "I am pleased to meet you face to face. And curiously, you are escorted by my wayward son. How odd. I cannot imagine how the fates have conspired to have your disparate paths cross. May I introduce my Royal Consultant, Cthonia? She is one of the original Feranith Sisters of the North. She has been with our family a long time and is my concubine."

King Uictore stopped speaking for a moment as his eyes became slits. He looked straight at Calyx.

"I am sorry, Warrior Queen, but you must understand that the Fae folk are not welcome here. In fact, I will not discuss business in front of your Fae companion. I am sure we can make her comfortable in an anteroom while the rest of us talk. Do you mind, Brynn, Daughter of the Electi?"

Brynn turned at looked at Calyx. For some reason, Calyx had a look of desperation in her eyes, though she remained mute. Brynn made a decision quickly. She didn't want to sweat the small stuff, and looking around she could see several derogatory banners hanging from the walls denigrating the Fairy race. One, written in Latin, said, *Death to the Tricksy Scoundrels.*

Looking back at Uictore, she nodded in agreement.

"Wait for us," she said to Calyx.

A veiled woman dressed like a servant motioned Calyx to follow her out of the Reception chambers. All eyes followed Calyx, including the eyes of Uictore, until she disappeared behind the velvet curtains on the opposite side of the room.

"Now," Uictore said, "I want you to tell me why you have come here, Warrior Queen of the Electi, when we are sworn enemies."

CHAPTER EIGHTEEN:
BATTERED & BRUISED

"My turn," the Liquidator standing at the side of the table with several companions complained in a loud voice, "Don't ever get Fairy Ass around here. I want a taste."

The huge, ugly man on top of Calyx gave one last grunt and shove for emphasis before he withdrew and tucked his cock back behind the folds of his lace-up soldier's breeches. The slight female with matted blonde hair who had been underneath him barely stirred as she lay completely naked and spread-eagled on the rough planks of one end of the dining table in the Soldier's barracks of the Liquidators.

Eyes glittering, the unkempt companion of the soldier that had just finished fucking Calyx, licked his lips as he surveyed her naked body.

"She's a pretty one," he said, letting out

his breath with a whistle at the end. "She got two, you know. Two of what the fair sex hide between their legs. Why don't we turn her on her side and both go at her, one from the front and the other from behind? Double team her hot Fairy quim, I say. Fairies is made for fucking. That's just a fucking fact."

As he plunged into her, another of the soldiers reached over to grab her breasts, and another flipped her on her side so that he might penetrate her second vagina. Still another, more agile man leaped on top of the table and kneeling with Calyx's head between his knees, opened her cupid bow mouth and inserted the head of his member between her lips.

"Ah," he said, exhaling raggedly. "I wish you hadn't struck her so hard. If she were awake, I'd have her suck on my Johnson."

The next few minutes passed as the rest of the Liquidators assigned to King Uictore's Private Guard took turns pleasuring themselves. Finally, after an hour, a tall woman, with waist-length black hair opened the door to the room, flanked by two servants.

"Your fun is over," she announced, "Get off of her now. Lettie and Mazie," she continued, turning to the servants, "clean her up, redress her in her clothing, and hurry. I think King Uictore has made a decision."

Calyx moaned. The servants hazily washed her off with dampened linen cloths, replaced her clothing, and carried her away from the Soldier's quarters, each one with an arm under her armpit. Calyx's tiny feet barely touched the floor.

"Here," the black-haired Witch Cthonia told them, "take her to my private dressing room. I have smelling salts in there."

Once Calyx was sat in a damask-covered chair in the corner, Cthonia quickly rooted through a cabinet, at last finding a small, stoppered bottle of green liquid. She took out the stopper and held it directly underneath Calyx's small nose. Calyx's eyes began to flutter as she simultaneously began coughing. She was alert within a few seconds.

"What happened?" she asked while scrabbling for the dagger at her side that was no longer there.

Cthonia bent and looked into her eyes, her beautiful brow puckered with concern.

"I believe you fainted, my love," she said in a soothing voice. "But you are back with us now!"

In the Reception Chambers of King Uictore of the Liquidators, there was a momentary silence as Brynn readied herself to answer the obvious question the King had posed.

"I have come on behalf of my people and my race," she said, speaking loudly and evenly. "To request that you cease your direct attacks on our stronghold. None have been successful. The Electi have proven more than your equals and rebuffed every campaign you have launched against us. Surely you must tire of losing both soldiers and reputation in defeat after defeat. I propose a Truce. As you know, our philosophies are diametrically opposed, and the Electi disdain, and that is a mild term, your activities. But it is a big planet, even in these modern times."

King Uictore seemed to consider all Brynn had said.

"What do you propose to offer us if we do agree to your proposal, Oh Daughter of the Electi?" he asked. "You know our troops are without number. You also know that we have limitless means of replenishing them, that they live for spoils of war, and that they seek only their enemy's blood. What you consider defeats, we consider victories. Why? Because just as a torrent at the mouth of a river erodes the soil, we are breaking down your defenses bit by bit. Warrior Queen, you are formidable and have no peer in battle. But as you stand before me, I perceive that you still have the weakness of your sex — a woman's heart. That alone is enough to prove your undoing."

Brynn bristled and chose to disregard his unkind remarks.

"I bring you your son," she responded, loudly enough so that her voice echoed off the stone surround. "Your own mongrel son, Creed. We will leave him in exchange for an agreement and for the return of certain artifacts that your Liquidator troops pillaged from my Father's castle when my sister

Gwenyth and I were children. All of those artifacts of the Electi are meaningless to you."

The King stroked his beard.

"You have something of ours, as I recall," he replied, "The First Sigil? Ring a bell, Daughter of the Electi?"

Brynn hesitated. The fact that the Electi owned the flag of the Liquidators that they had surrendered in the first ancient battle was a great source of inspiration and power for the Electi and had been for centuries. She had never expected that it would be included in any negotiations. King Uictore continued speaking, gesturing to Creed.

"Why should I want this ruin of a warrior back?" he said disdainfully. "With one glance I can see that he has become nothing more than the lapdog of Brynn, Daughter of the Electi. He would be of no use to me. I can discern that he has his whore mother's weaknesses. He disgusts me. The only reason I would consider him as a bargaining chip is so that I could wipe him out of existence. That wouldn't be worth the energy it takes to swing my sword over his head," Uictore spat, glaring at Creed as he continued. "I have never missed you, Bastard. All your life you defied me and brought me shame. Now that I see that you have ended up the pet and slave to a Daughter of the Electi, I am not in the least surprised. It may surprise you to know that I have sired many children after you, all of them fine sons of whom I am proud. Let me introduce them to you."

As King Uictore waved his arm in a
sweeping gesture, five young men stepped out
of the ranks surrounding the throne. Two of
them bore an uncanny resemblance to Creed.
All of them had blond hair varying in shades
from dishwater to silver-white.

"Let me present my legitimate sons —
the eldest is Cristo, the next is Broslyn, in the
middle is Ferute, then Vagare, and my
youngest, Tallye."

Creed could not help but show surprise
on his handsome face. He had heard rumors
that he had half-brothers through the years,
but that was par for the course with Kings in
any realm. They were all rutting fools who
produced dozens of offspring both recognized
and unrecognized. Creed was half-surprised
there weren't more of them.

For some reason, his eyes locked with
the youngest of them, the one King Uictore
had introduced as Tallye. The young man,
with hair like quicksilver past his shoulders,
winked at Creed. Creed had no idea what to
make of it.

Suddenly, Uictore clapped his hands
together, and servants came scurrying, setting
up long tables for the dinner meal.

"We shall all dine together while the
Warrior Queen Brynn considers my offers. I
pledge to you that nothing is poisoned and
that the simple fare will be to your taste —
mostly pheasant and ducking and other
wildfowl, but avoid the fricassee. I am afraid it
has human meat in it. Though you really

should try it. After all, it is a small step to go from enjoying the blood to feasting on the flesh."

For some reason, King Uictore's remark brought down the house, most of the population of Liquidator guards and subjects roaring with laughter.

Brynn gave the others a look as if to say, "Avoid the fricassee." When she turned, a dazed Calyx appeared at her elbow, dressed in a satin gown with ribbons in her hair.

"Calyx," Brynn practically shouted. "Where are your weapons?"

Calyx lifted her gown. Brynn could see that, other than Calyx's sword, all her weapons were strapped to her thigh.

"Brynn, I think they may have drugged me," Calyx told her in a low voice. "They say I fainted, but that was impossible. When I awakened, that Witch Cthonia was standing over me with smelling salts."

"Well, never mind if you are okay," Brynn told her. "Though I will certainly ask after your sword. Thank God it wasn't your good one."

When they were all seated, King Uictore raised a glass of wine, and everyone except Brynn and her entourage joined him in a Liquidator blessing over the meal. Calyx waited until they had served themselves and one by one, passed their plates under her delicate nostrils. Because she was a Fairy, she had a built-in poison detector and acted as their official tester for the group in case their

Liquidator host had somehow tainted the food he was offering.

Brynn, despite her instinctive hatred for Liquidators in general, was semi-impressed that Uictore had warned them about the dish containing human flesh. That was an unexpected courtesy since Uictore could very well have just watched them eat it for his amusement and then informed them afterward.

On the other side of Creed, who had made sure that he was next to her just as Tarren had, was the lad Tallye, Creed's newly introduced half-brother. As Creed nodded to him, he leaned over and whispered.

"Brother, Creed. I want to come with you. Please allow it."

Although Creed had inclined his ear to hear his half-brother better in the noise, background music, and general hubbub of the room, he quickly jerked back in surprise and consternation. He stared at the silver-haired young man, who had some of his own features, in disbelief.

"You had best keep to your own, Liquidator," he said in a low voice. "What would our father think of your boldness? Maybe I should stand and announce it now to win his favor?"

Tallye looked genuinely terrified.

"Oh, Brother, I beg you. I am both serious and desperate. I have heard that you were a rogue and a bloodthirsty one at that. But seeing that you have formed an alliance

254

with the Queen of Souls, the Amazing Daughter of the Electi Brynn sets my mind at ease regarding both your philosophy and purpose. I could be a boon to you both. I know many things that would advance your cause."

Creed looked nervously around him. He didn't see anyone noticing that he was even having a conversation with Tallye. Brynn herself seemed preoccupied with a conversation she and Tarren were having in which Tarren's face was becoming redder and redder, the veins on his neck standing out. Looking down into his filled pewter dinner plate, he said gruffly.

"Wait for us outside the Port door — the one hidden in the stone wall. Make your excuses, feign a stomachache, and give your regards to the King. Tell him you need to lie down and then wait for us."

He turned his head to the side, a smile creeping across his face.

"I sense you are sincere but do not disappoint me, or I will draw and quarter you from that oak tree near the port door. Do we understand each other, Tallye?"

"Aye, Brother Creed," the lad answered, his voice nearly a whisper. "You will not regret this. I promise you on my life."

"Yes," Creed returned, not looking at Tallye. "On your life. Remember that."

After a few more minutes of eating in silence, Tallye got up from his chair and made his way to the head of the table. Creed tuned in on the conversation between Brynn and

Tarren that seemed to have escalated.

"You have no choice," Brynn hissed. "And I will hear nothing else as your leader. Ye Gods, Tarren, you forget yourself."

Tarren, his face flushed darkly with unexpressed emotion, lowered his head. Creed could see that the Stalwart Protector of the Electi Queen had barely touched his food.

"As my Queen demands it of me, so shall it be done," he said, sighing deeply.

"And kiss my ring also," Brynn insisted, shoving it under his face. "So that I am sure you have acquiesced, Tarren."

Tarren made a noise in his throat but did as she asked.

"My Queen, Brynn, Daughter of the Electi, I give my word," he said, his shoulders slumped in defeat just as if she had beaten him in an actual sword battle.

Creed tapped Brynn on the shoulder, and she turned. Rather than looking distressed, as he expected, she looked pleased with herself.

"Brynn, what's up?" he asked, smiling at her.

Looking into her beautiful face, he forgave her everything, including using him as a pawn to try to get to his father.

"Everything is fine," she told him, smiling beatifically. "Tarren and Gwenyth are to be wed," she said to him, a knot of barely concealed triumph in her voice.

Just as the servants were clearing the table in preparation for dessert, Brynn felt a tap on her shoulder from behind. Her first reaction was to whirl and shout that she dared not be touched by the likes of the Liquidator swill, but she stopped herself. On either side of her, she felt Tarren and Creed both ready their weapons in response to someone being bold enough to dare touch her.

It was the Witch Cthonia.

"Ah, my apologies, Brynn, Daughter of the Electi," she responded, smiling, and giving a mock curtsey. "I was just curious to see if you were as soft as the rest of us females since you are worshiped as a Goddess. Do you know who I am?" the Witch added, bending down so that she could be face-to-face with Brynn.

"I know that you are King Uictore's Concubine in the Kingdom of the Liquidators. Though we would call you a common whore in the Kingdom of the Electi," Brynn said crisply, enunciating every word. "I also know you are rude, as you must surely recognize how crass it is to violate the purity of a Daughter of the Electi with your corrupt touch."

Cthonia sneered.

"Wrong answer, you stupid little pale cow," she said evenly. "I am the first female that ever fucked your new lover Creed. He couldn't get enough of me. Huge libido, that one."

"And you," she spat, turning to Creed, "I can smell Electi bitch all over you. No wonder the King despises you so."

The words were barely out of her bright red mouth when Brynn stood up and came toward Cthonia, knocking over the chair she'd been sitting in and drawing her sword.

"I am sorry for your words, Amazon Witch," Brynn said, her face instantly flushed with rage. "It is my mission to remove that tongue that gave them utterance, but since I am not one to worry about precision I think it will serve me just as well to use a broad stroke to sever your spiteful head from your shoulders."

Brynn waited only for a page to run up to Cthonia with a sword before shrilling a war cry that echoed from all four walls and striking with her sword. Around Brynn and Cthonia, a large space had been cleared for the fight, with tables pushed back to make plenty of room.

Creed, Tarren, and Bayn all stood at the ready. If this were to be a one-on-one battle between the women, they had no cause to join in unless it escalated.

With the first deadly accurate stroke, Brynn partially severed the Witch's head from her long neck, the blade making a long deep cut from the side nearly severing it and shortening Cthonia's hair into a more modern style incidentally. To Brynn's horror, rather than toppling over, Cthonia cracked her neck to one side, then the other, healing the laceration instantly. The first thing Cthonia did after that was look down on the flagstones beneath her feet. One-half of her long hair lay splayed against the stonework.

"The *bitchtress* ruined my beautiful hair," she shouted, "and will die for it along with her insolence."

"And you all seem to forget that you have broken the treaty on more than one occasion, and we have been rather lenient by not showing up here before now. Rather peacefully, I might add." Brynn held her arms out to the side in a show of bravado. "Because of that, you are free to make the first move, but know this. I will kill you and the rest of your Liquidator filth will follow."

She swung her own sword just as Brynn raised hers to meet it, and a powerful clanging sound rang out. The ear-splitting noise of well-forged metal striking metal could be heard for the next five seconds. Frustrated, Cthonia took a swing that caught Brynn on the outside of her thigh. Though her blood ran, Brynn felt the healing of the angel blood she had consumed earlier working its magic. With a fizzing sound, her wounds closed much more quickly than they normally did with her natural vampire propensity for healing.

Again Brynn struck Cthonia, this time on the side of the head, slicing one of her ears off. It instantly wriggled up Cthonia's neck and back into position, looking like a slug and leaving a viscous bloody trail. Brynn shot a desperate look over to Creed, Tarren, and

Bayn. Creed seemed to be trying to communicate something.

He was touching his right eye.

Sweat-soaked from her exertions, Brynn turned back to Cthonia, spinning, and sticking the point of her sword as far as it would go into Cthonia's right eye. She then pulled it out before she landed with a thump on the floor. For just a moment, the witch teetered, and then reached out blindly in front of her as if her sight were gone.

"King Uictore," she shouted. "Avenge me."

Uictore's features twisted in pure rage and anger as well as something Brynn didn't think the Liquidator King was capable of. Grief. Immediately, the chamber filled with bodies gyrating and clashing against each other in the ancient death dance of war. Brynn looked around desperately for her Royal Guard who had been waiting patiently behind the velvet curtain. They were still there, but she couldn't have known that they'd been slain to a man several minutes earlier, their bodies dismembered completely, their flesh laying in chunks to be collected by the cook for the next fricassee.

Altogether, given their superior fighting skills, the Electi were more than a match for the Liquidators even though they were outnumbered three to one. Brynn felt desperate though — being in Castle Crimayne meant there could be thousands of them.

Calyx cut off the head of the Liquidator

standing between herself and Brynn.

"I have one, yes. Tell me when to throw it," Calyx said.

Brynn nodded. She waited until she was sure that all of their backs were facing the exit that the group had used to come in. She then whistled over to Calyx. Calyx instantly threw up what looked like a tangled ball of wire into the air. Once aloft, the wire expanded outward in all directions, floating above the sea of Liquidator soldiers for a nanosecond before descending like a shroud over them. Then there were sizzling sounds, unholy screams, and flashes of blue lightning emanating off the metallic net.

"I smell fried Liquidator," Brynn smirked as they made their escape.

It was uncharacteristic of her that she couldn't see if King Uictore were dead or alive through the soldier's bodies, but every instinct she had was telling her that if they remained in the hall, they would be slaughtered. She had already done the math.

They ran feverishly outside, and then beyond the wall that they had cleared when they first ventured in. Then they took to the air.

Brynn flew along companionably next to Creed when suddenly she caught sight of the being on the other side of him. The man's his long silver hair fluttered behind him, glistening in the abundant moonlight. The youth turned to smile and nod at her, and she was instantly furious.

"Down now!" she screamed at all of them, before plunging headfirst down to terra firma, righting herself at the last minute and reaching solid ground before any of the rest of them.

The first thing she did since she was too out of breath to speak, was slap Creed across the face as hard as she could.

"How dare you!" she blurted when she'd caught her breath, "bring a Liquidator with us. Unacceptable. I don't care if he is your brother."

Having gotten out only half of what she'd wanted to say, and because it pissed her off that she had to pause in speaking in order to catch her breath, Brynn hit Creed in the face for emphasis.

"What the Hell are you even thinking, mongrel?" she demanded.

Creed recognized that it was a rhetorical question, but he decided to seize the opening she had given him before she started hitting him again. He also wondered how many times he would have to fuck her before she stopped calling him *mongrel*. He couldn't wait to find out.

"With all due respect, Queen Warrior Brynn, Daughter of the Electi, I sincerely believe that my half-brother Tallye will be an asset to us. He has insider information that will give us an edge. He knows what campaigns they have been planning well into the future and what their objectives are in each one. Plus, even though he is a mite shorter, he looks a lot like me, which gives me a particular fondness for him. He is strong and has been aptly trained in the Warring arts. He is prepared to pledge fealty to you and only to you in whichever way you choose to test him."

Brynn turned to face Tallye. Though he loomed over her, the energy emanating from her was so formidable he found himself thoroughly intimidated.

"Are you prepared to show me fealty by facing any test I might require of you?" she asked the handsome blond man standing before her in a quietly menacing tone. "I might scourge the skin off your back. Will you suffer for me? Will you worship me as your queen? Will you do my bidding always?" she finished.

Tallye knelt on one knee before her.

"Yes my liege, Brynn, Daughter of the Electi. I am prepared to face whatever I must to serve you. I have admired you from afar all my life. The tales of your bravery are legendary, your swordplay is matchless, and your beauty is renowned all over the Earth. I have prayed to join you since childhood, and I will not disappoint you."

As he remained there with his head bowed, a smile began to play around Brynn's lips.

"That will do for now," she muttered. "When we return I will ask our Oracle Natalia to prepare an induction ceremony for you. You will be marked to my service with a permanent mark, one that will designate you the property of the Electi. A mark so striking that it will mean your instant death if you ever attempt to return to Crimayne and your vile Liquidator Father. Do you still accept my terms?"

Tallye raised his head. She was surprised that his eyes were an unusual green color. She had never seen a Liquidator with irises of such a rare hue.

"I swear, oath, and pledge that I do accept all your conditions, Queen of Warriors. I thank you for your trust in me."

Even as she motioned the kneeling lad to rise, Brynn laughed harshly.

"Tallye, son of Uictore, I have no trust to give you. Only pain and trial by fire. If you survive, you may find that your decision is more of a curse than a blessing. I may accept you into my service, but I intend to break you first."

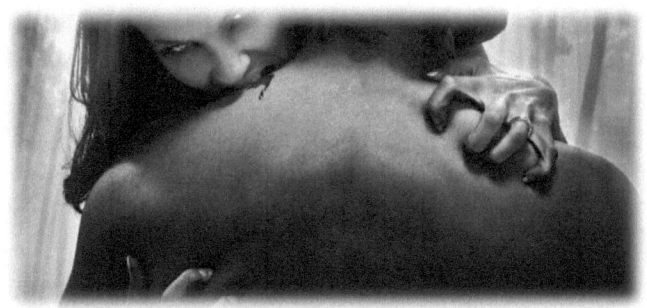

CHAPTER NINETEEN:
PREPARE FOR A STORM

They reached the Electi Manse in record time after that. Tallye seemed elated to even be traveling with them, though Brynn, Tarren, and Bayn had insisted that he not be allowed to have possession of even one weapon. Creed found himself looking both at Tallye and then at Brynn. He wondered what was going on in her head. He had taken a liking to Tallye — felt instinctive that his younger half-brother's motives were pure. At the same time, he knew the legendary propensity for cruelty ran deeply in Brynn's royal veins, and he shuddered for what she might put Tallye, a Liquidator turncoat through before she was satisfied and assured of his complete loyalty.

He had claimed her, and it had been a victory so sweet nothing in his existence could or ever would match it. At the same time, he knew that everyone in Brynn's Inner circle had endured torture of one kind or another to earn the privilege of being close to her.

If the truth be told, he feared for Tallye.

Despite the two maidservants holding her hands, one patting the withered and gloved hand and the other holding Gwenyth's perfect one, as Gwenyth sat in a huge armchair in her chambers anticipating the return of her sister Queen Brynn, she quaked with fear.

Other emotions took turns within her fragile body. Part of her was furious beyond reason at Brynn for hunting Ryder down like a dog. Another part of her was suffused with guilt that Ryder's fondness for her had placed him in danger for his life. Then there was the deep sense of shame she felt for letting her emotions cloud her reason, for not reckoning the consequences of her wanton passion for the first real male entity she had ever been with.

Of all of her emotions, the shame ran most deeply, and she knew that whatever Brynn decided her consequence should be she would be forced to bear it without argument.

Brynn had always been the best role model for her, Gwenyth reasoned. Brynn had never realized that she was cut from an entirely different cloth. She had never had the strength of will and self-discipline of a real leader, and Brynn had proven herself over and over to be not only a leader, but also the true savior of the Electi.

There was a knock at the door, startling Gwenyth out of her dark thoughts. She sensed Brynn on the other side and closed her eyes to take a steadying breath before facing her older sister. The maidservant to her right looked to her for guidance, never asking the question out loud. Everyone knew she was to face a punishment handed down to her by the Warrior Queen and Gwenyth knew that because she was her sister, her punishment would be harsher than any Brynn could pass on to anyone else within the Electi. This was the reason she hesitated slightly before replying.

"You may let her in. Whatever she has planned will happen now or later so it may as well be now," she said as she rose from her chair.

Gwenyth smoothed the front of her dress as the maidservant moved to the door and let Brynn inside the room. The scent that came with Brynn was unmistakable. Not only could you still smell Creed's claim on her, but other aromas mingled with it, making it nearly unpalatable. Brynn didn't hug her younger sister, which was typical of them. Instead, she stood before her with a hand on her elegantly curving hip and pinned Gwenyth with her crimson stare. Gwenyth scrunched her face as the underlying smell of burning flesh nearly smothered everything else.

"It is done, sister. You have been avenged," Brynn stated proudly with her chest pushed out with pride in her accomplishment.

"You stink of death, Brynn," was all Gwenyth knew to say.

Brynn smiled and turned away from her sister to sit on the plush chair across from her, crossing one leg over the other as she sat with her arms resting on the armrests. She looked like a true queen then. Gwenyth couldn't deny that.

"It is an unfortunate side effect of killing that traitor. I'm certain I will stink of it for weeks."

Gwenyth turned away from her sister as tears stung her eyes. She wiped them away with a gloved finger and followed suit, sitting in the chair so she could look her older sister in the eye for the first time since the incident.

"I'm sorry, dear Gwenyth. If I had any other choice—"

"You had plenty of options. Do not feel sorry for me."

"I will tell you this, Ryder's intentions were not as pure as he led you to believe. When I found him, he was on his way to Crimayne with your parcel in his hand. He was taking it to the Liquidator king, Uictore. For what purpose, it is still unclear, but I will get down to the bottom of it. I can promise you that."

Shock and disbelief moved through Gwenyth's frail body in waves, a chill running through her that she fought to hide. She would remain strong in the face of her older sister, Queen, and judge.

"And I take it you spoke with Uictore?" Gwenyth questioned.

"I did," Brynn replied with a nod.

"And?"

"And nothing. Nothing came of the meeting once the witch in his court challenged me. Uictore completely disregards the treaty of 1514, so we have no choice but to declare full-on war against the Liquidators."

Gwenyth said nothing, unsure if there was anything she could say to her sister. The war with the Liquidators had always been in the forefront of her mind. That and collecting the Quaji to replenish their ranks. That was until lately even though she was certain the war still raged inside of Brynn with the same ferocity.

Brynn jumped up and stretched out a hand toward Gwenyth.

"Come walk with me awhile, dear sister," she said smiling. "We can talk more, and there is something I would like you to see."

Gwenyth did as she was told, though she didn't trust the gleam in her older sister's eye. She found it odd that Brynn could play the pristine and virginal Warrior Goddess one minute, and the next minute let a Liquidator Mongrel ravish her. The fact that Creed also had angelic blood seemed no excuse for Brynn's recent assignation with Creed. And it was her misfortune as the younger Daughter of the Electi that Brynn was allowed to matchmake for her as if she had no right to choose for herself.

Gwenyth thought they might be heading to the labyrinth or the white rose garden. Instead, she opened the massive front door, looking behind her only once to make sure Gwenyth followed. The night air was refreshing, the moon turning the treetops to silver as they walked out across the vast marble porch with its stout columns and down the broad steps of the entranceway to the manse.

Their feet crunched on the gravel of the circular drive, and Gwenyth wondered where they were going. Down the driveway to the city street? Was she taking her to Starbucks? Abruptly Brynn stopped and turned to her, turning her around with her hands firmly on Gwenyth's small shoulders.

With a feeling of dread in her gut, Gwenyth turned. The spectacular Hollywood-style exterior lights of the manse crisscrossed over the upper third of the impressive structure. And then in the apex of the beams of light, in the center of the third-floor balcony that opened off Brynn's chambers, she saw it.

Ryder's head was fastened to one of the talons of the iron dragon that graced Brynn's balcony, crouched there as a ward for the manse, a gargoyle that was coiled to attack.

Gwenyth's scream was cut short when Brynn, standing slightly behind her, clamped a hand still soiled by battle over her younger sister's mouth.

"There he is, Gwenyth, darling. Your traitorous lover. And there he shall remain until the last of him is picked away by the crows. He is not so handsome or charming now, is he? Yet, you let him defile you. Well I, your older sister, avenged you. He shall never brag that he was intimate with you, or that he despoiled you. Not only did I sever his head from his body, I cut out his tongue. And you are to marry Tarren to cover up your idiocy, sister. You have no choice."

Gwenyth began to quiver. As terrible a sight as Ryder's head was, she felt frozen in place, unable to look away. Her knees felt weak, as though they might give way at any moment.

Brynn removed her hand from Gwenyth's mouth, but Gwenyth, filled with a horror that placed her beyond the capacity for all speech, did not make a single sound. Brynn reached her hand in between her sister's small breasts, noticing the chain that held what was left of Ryder beside a corpse. Her fingers entwined in the gold. She pulled it up and out of its hiding place under Gwenyth's dress, bringing it up into the moonlight as she came around to stand before her, rage evident in her posture. With one quick jerk, the chain snapped from around Gwenyth's slender neck as Brynn removed it with so much force the metal rubbed painfully into her flesh.

"This is further proof of the disgrace you have caused our house, and you will not keep it," Brynn chided as she closed the pendant in a tight fist.

"But... sister—"

Instantly, Gwenyth's cheek stung and shock ran through her. Brynn had never touched her with such force in her entire life, always coddling her because of her deformity and how others treated her. With wide eyes, she stared at her older sister who had clearly had enough of her stupidity and her betrayal.

"That is enough, Gwyn. Enough. You nearly cost all of us our lives. I am not just your sister. I am your Queen, and you will do as I say or suffer the consequences. Do you understand me?"

Gwenyth was stunned into silence, but knew better than to answer. Brynn turned on her heel at her sister's muteness and walked back into the mansion, leaving her young sister to watch in horror.

"I think Gwenyth got the message," Brynn said. towel drying her hair as she emerged from her steamy and grand bathroom, with its Egyptian marble tiling and extra appointments like an enormous sunken bathtub and a bidet.

She wore a fluffy white robe, but had left it open in the front. Creed, who had been lounging on her bed waiting for her to emerge, looked her up and down appraisingly.

"I think you are breathtaking, Brynn,

Queen Warrior of the Electi. And sometimes a bit harsh, to be honest," he told her, though his eyes were sympathetic.

He understood the weight of responsibility that rested on Brynn's shoulders from an early age, and he thought he understood why she had developed a well-deserved reputation for cruelty. She needed that reputation to keep her enemies at bay.

Brynn looked into his eyes for a long moment, the golden sparkles in her crimson eyes were dancing in the soft light of her chambers.

"You don't know my younger sister," she told him. "It will take all that and more to convince her that she is not capable of choosing a mate wisely. Her foolishness nearly cost us everything. I had to find a way to drive that point home. I know that you think I am without compassion for her youth and inexperience, but you couldn't be more wrong, Creed. She and I are very different in our ability to judge character. I had more wisdom at the age of five than she has even now. We do share the passionate natures of the Daughters of the Electi, but hers is an open, yearning heart that will only invite wolves into our fold."

"And?" Creed said, patting the place on the bed next to him.

He was losing focus, staring at the parts of her luscious body that were revealed beyond the open robe she half-wore. It distracted him to the point of torture.

"I told her she is to marry Tarren, and as soon as possible." Brynn finished, allowing the beautiful robe to drop from her shoulders onto the floor.

She stood there, more beautiful than the neoclassical paintings of Venus that graced the walls of the foyer of the residence, resplendently voluptuous in all the places that mattered.

"Hmmmm," was the only answer Creed could make as his eyes devoured her.

His manhood rose to tent the towel he had casually thrown around his hips alarmingly. He reached out his arm. She took his hand and allowed him to pull her down beside him into the shadow of his glowing, burnished muscular body.

He kissed her longingly and passionately, her tongue snaking in between his parted lips. A masculine and animal groan forced its way out of his chest, Brynn responding with gyrating hips as she wrapped her legs around him and turned him so that he rested in the cradle of her body. She gasped as she felt his arousal push into her core, opening her crimson eyes to stare into his, smirking seductively.

"Looks like someone is happy to see me," she said, her voice low and husky with lust.

"Oh, I'm more than happy," he replied as he leaned down to nuzzle into the curve of her throat, biting hard enough to make her nails dig into his back and a soft sigh to leave her.

His tongue flicked out and licked her earlobe, breaths coming hard and fast.

"I'm going to fuck you harder than you beat me, my love," he whispered.

She gasped playfully and pulled away to look at him. The excitement was alight in her eyes, which only excited him even more.

"Oh, I did not beat you that hard, you buffoon," she giggled.

He chuckled at her.

"That's why I said *harder*."

"Hmmmm, you promise?"

With one swift motion, he removed the towel from his hips, threw it to the floor, and turned Brynn over onto her stomach. The water from her wet hair made her skin glisten seductively. He leaned down and licked up her back, tasting the sweet fragrance she used in the rivulet of water running down her elegant posterior. He couldn't wait any longer to be inside of her and knew that if he continued to play the small games she seemed to enjoy he'd finish without being inside of her for even a second. With his nose buried in the nape of her neck again, he found her opening with his erection. She was soft, warm, welcoming, and so wet he could slip inside so easily.

"Always," he whispered into her ear.

He slammed into her, barely taking a moment to think about doing anything other than being enveloped by her, completely and utterly. She cried out in pure ecstasy and reached back to grip his backside to pull him in deeper. He moved inside of her, giving her everything he had including his mind and soul. Everything belonged to her. Anything he could give her he would.

Pleasure rippled through them both, and he felt her shudder underneath him and around him, rocking her hips as he rocked against her. Each stroke roared through his entire body and crashed into him like a tidal wave. He reached around and took one of her beautiful breasts in his large hand, caressing her nipple until it stood erect against his palm. His teeth grazed her shoulder, and he heard her growl, deep, feral, and rumbling. It made him want to move within her even faster and even harder.

She turned her head slightly, and her gaze met his, alight with a ferocious lust that almost caused him to lose complete control of his faculties.

"Feed from me, Creed. Take what belongs to you," she purred as another stroke sent a delicious wave of pleasure through the both of them.

She closed her eyes and her lips parted. Without a second thought, the vampire inside of him roared to the surface and he sunk his fangs into the bend of her neck, the iron tang of her sweet blood hitting his tongue. Before he knew it he was on his back, and she straddled him, her beautiful body hovered over his erection as she did so. Brynn took him into her hand and placed his head against her, lowering onto him with such slowness he greedily grabbed her hips and shoved her down onto his shaft completely.

Once he was entirely inside of her, she moved on top of him. Her breasts were high and tight with her arousal, and she bit her full bottom lip as she moved on top of him with a continuous swivel of her hips. They both rode the height of their passion in perfect sync as their bodies drove their actions.

He watched with fascination as her hand traveled to stroke herself. She leaned her head back and sighed as her body contracted around him, another shock of pure and animal lust shuddering through him. Her breathing quickened in step with his own, and they climbed higher and higher until they both cried out as their passion came to its peak.

Creed filled her with his seed as her softness convulsed around him. His hands gripped her hips, and he drove himself as deep into her as he could, wanting her to have everything he could give her. She collapsed on top of him as they both breathed and attempted to catch their breaths.

And it wasn't until that moment that Creed felt he had found where he actually belonged.

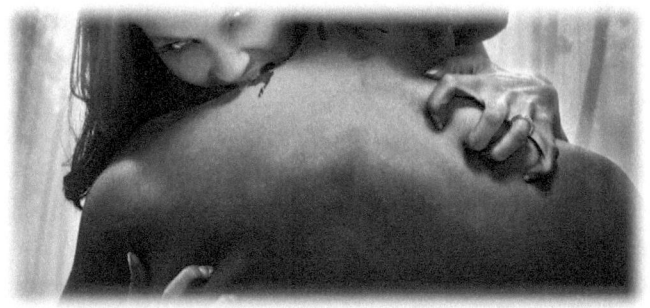

CHAPTER TWENTY
REFLECTIONS

Alone at last in her chambers, Gwenyth stifled her cries by burying her face into one of her immense bed pillows. It was bad enough Brynn had beheaded the first man to ever pay attention to her. At least that was somewhat understandable if what everyone said was true, that Ryder had been headed to Crimayne to pledge loyalty to King Uictore, but the fact that she was being given to Tarren before her wounded young heart had even had a chance to heal was another matter indeed.

It wasn't fair. It wasn't her fault to be born after Brynn, but she felt that she had paid for her unfortunate position of Younger Daughter all of her life and was still paying.

Involuntarily, her fingers traveled to the place between her young breasts where the necklace Ryder had given her had rested the past few months. Gwenyth had used it as a touchstone. Just knowing it was there reassured her that she was desirable in spite of her withered arm and that she had won the heart of at least one male entity.

Now it was gone. Brynn had ripped it off her neck as soon as she had returned, recognizing immediately that it must have been a secret gift from her former love. When Gwenyth had protested, she had struck her across the face for the first time in both their lives, telling her that she had nearly cost them all their lives.

She also told her she was to be given to Tarren, a male entity that she had grown up with. Tarren was handsome, to be sure, and had always been kind to her, treating her as a big brother would treat a little sister. She had always known he was in love with her sister, and that knowledge alone was enough to keep her from ever developing even a schoolgirl crush on him.

At that moment in time, she only hoped Tarren would understand her apprehension even though she was confident he felt the same way about the arrangement. Her eyes burned with tears of frustration, grief over Ryder, and genuine fear that he would reject her. Granted, she had never seen him in a romantic light, but being rejected hurt no matter who was responsible.

She wiped one tear that escaped down her cheek with her gloved hand and hoped that, beyond the shadow of a doubt, her naïveté would disappear, and she could finally stand up to her older sister's cruelty.

Creed lay beside Brynn in the darkness offered by the thick curtains to protect them from the morning sunlight. A minuscule amount of light shone in a line just at the base of the thick fabric, but not enough to reach them.

Brynn slept soundlessly beside him as he watched, her arms cradling her head and lying on her flat stomach. She had kicked the blankets off her body, leaving him to feel the lust roll within him like a brush fire once again. But he would let her sleep. She had gone through enough over the last few days and needed to prepare to endure even more with her stature as Queen of the Electi.

He would be by her side as her King.

As gingerly as he could, he reached out and traced his fingers along her spine in soft caresses. She didn't stir, not even as muscles twitched underneath his touch. He couldn't help but think about how drastically everything had changed since he invaded the Electi's stronghold, his dark and dominating obsession with the legendary warrior Queen turning to pure and unadulterated love that he felt so deeply it would never leave him.

His father had known about his obsession long before the moment he infiltrated his own stronghold with Brynn at his side. Uictore had even hoped the call of battle would be enough to satiate that obsession, taking its place entirely, but there was no such luck for the Liquidator King. The man wanted nothing more than for the mighty House of Electi to fall under his power.

Creed vowed to himself as he continued to watch his love slumber deeply after their lovemaking that he wouldn't allow that to transpire. He would protect his Queen and her people, his people, with his life. Without hesitation.

Some distance away, a forgotten being with a score to settle made its way toward the manse of the warrior Queen of the Electi.

ABOUT THE AUTHORS

KINDRA SOWDER resides with her family in South Carolina. She holds two advanced degrees in Criminal Neuropsychology and she obtained her Master's in Literature, emphasizing in Creative Writing and Fiction, recently. While she would like to say her life is boring, it is not with her always on the go husband and the perpetual lack of sleep due to her toddler, not to mention a very furry and somewhat clumsy, ninja assassin Maine Coon. Her works have earned multiple awards and nominations.

To keep up with Kindra Sowder:
Website: www.ksowderauthor.com
Facebook: Kindra Sowder
Twitter: @kindrakinnaman
Instagram: @ksowderauthor
LinkedIn: Kindra Sowder
Amazon: Kindra Sowder

P MATTERN is a USA Today, Award winning, RONE Award nominated and Bestselling Author of over 140 books and Novellas in genres of Thriller, Horror and Paranormal romance, currently published by Book Nook Nuts, LLC, Tell-Tale Publishing and Dark Books Press, best known for her *Full Moon Series*, *Vampire Princess Series, Midnight Magnolias Saga* and *The Creatures Who Love Me Series*.

Amazon Author Page
        Https://www.amazon.com/stores/P.-Mattern/author/B00MYKZCXY
Facebook
        http://bit.ly/2BXVCZm

Book 2 of
The Liquidator
Wars
Coming Soon!